can be a pretty persuasive guy…”

suasive or not, the farm has to stay a farm or ot selling. That’s my sticking point,” Jenna l.

1… Maybe I’ll just have to try … e out get you unstuck…”

luck wit… the flirting i…

hed. “It … you, Jenna Bo…

o,” Jenna responded.

meet the man who would very likely be ental in dashing her late father’s one wish?

vasn’t sure how that could be.

’t I tell you?” Meg whispered from beside he left. “He’s nice, isn’t he?”

e to look at,” was all Jenna would admit, le a part of her acknowledged that she had d him quite a bit…

Dear Reader,

Loss and chaos have shaken Jenna Bowen in the past eleven months. Desperate to find some calm for herself and her fifteen-month-old adopted daughter, she's returned to her hometown of Northbridge, Montana, where she's sure the last of the chaos will pass and she and Abby can settle into being a family of two.

Ian Kincaid is a dynamic man, raised—along with his estranged twin brother—by a legendary football powerhouse. Ian has spent his life earning his place as the legend's adopted son.

Jenna's unfortunate circumstances and Ian doing his father's bidding bring them together. On opposite sides of things, something still manages to click between them and before he knows what's hit him, Ian wants Jenna's family of two to be a family of three. Jenna isn't so sure about that idea. On the other hand, there's just something about the man…

Come see how it turns out.

Happy reading!

Victoria Pade

BIG SKY BRIDE, BE MINE!

BY
VICTORIA PADE

First published in Great Britain 2013
by Mills & Boon, an imprint of Harlequin (UK) Limited,
Eton House, 18-24 Paradise Road, Richmond, Surrey TW9 1SR

ISBN: 978 0 263 90080 4
ebook ISBN: 978 1 472 00436 9

23-0113

Harlequin (UK) policy is to use papers that are natural, renewable and recyclable products and made from wood grown in sustainable forests. The logging and manufacturing processes conform to the legal environmental regulations of the country of origin.

Printed and bound in Spain
by Blackprint CPI, Barcelona

Victoria Pade is a *USA TODAY* bestselling author of numerous romance novels. She has two beautiful and talented daughters—Cori and Erin—and is a native of Colorado, where she lives and writes. A devoted chocolate lover, she's in search of the perfect chocolate-chip cookie recipe. For information about her latest and upcoming releases, and to find recipes for some of the decadent desserts her characters enjoy, log on to www.vikkipade.com.

Chapter One

"Oh, look—this is where Mom hid J.J.'s princess costume!" Jenna Bowen exclaimed when she discovered the pint-size, ruffly, flouncy dress in the back of the hall closet she was clearing out.

"I remember that Halloween," Meg Perry-McKendrick said.

They were both on the floor. Jenna was on her knees scooting in and out of the closet, while her best friend since childhood held a garbage bag and a cardboard box in front of her, awaiting Jenna's decision about whether what she dragged out went to charity or into the trash.

Jenna sat back on her heels to hold up the costume she'd just discovered.

"We were sixteen that year," Meg continued. "I remember because we'd both had our driver's licenses for just a few weeks and neither of our parents would let us drive that night for fear we might hit a trick-or-treater.

We thought that was crazy. So, since we were sixteen, that would have made J.J. what? Four?"

"Four, right," Jenna confirmed, quickly calculating the age her much younger sister would have been at the time. "And instead of driving around, we ended up taking J.J. out. Rather than saying trick or treat at every door she regally stood there—"

"Just waiting to be given her due," Meg concluded as they both laughed at the shared memory.

"She was so cute," Jenna said affectionately. "But Mom couldn't get her out of this thing even after Halloween. She'd only change into her princess pajamas to go to bed at night. Mom would wash the costume while J.J. was asleep, hoping she'd get tired of wearing it the next day. But by Christmas, Mom couldn't take it anymore, and one morning when J.J. went looking for it, Mom said the washing machine had eaten it. I always figured she just threw it away, but apparently, she hid it in here."

"She was probably afraid J.J. would refuse to wear anything at all if she couldn't have the costume, so she'd better keep it, just in case. That's what I'd do if it were Tia."

Tia was the daughter of Meg's new husband.

"J.J. did spend that whole day in the house, in her pajamas," Jenna said. "Mom and Dad were worried she was going to start wearing those night and day, because one way or another, she insisted that she *was* a princess."

"J.J. always was strong willed and determined," Meg recalled.

Because she'd been around Jenna's house so much growing up, Meg knew the goings-on in the Bowen family as well as Jenna did. Jenna was packing up her family home, and since Meg had some free Saturday afternoon time, she'd come by to help.

With that bit of reminiscence over, Meg said, "Shall we save the costume for Abby? Think she'll take her turn at wanting to be a princess, too?"

"I have to streamline, remember?" Jenna answered. "That means, get rid of everything that isn't necessary, because I won't have room for more than Abby and I need. And after so many washings, the costume is pretty worn out. I don't think it can even go in the charity box. Let's just put it in the trash."

Meg took the costume from Jenna and complied by jamming the worn garment into the black plastic bag. Jenna crawled partially into the closet once again and grabbed up an entire pile of old sweaters from the floor.

"These are Mom's—they should all go to charity," Jenna said as she shifted from her knees to sit cross-legged so she could help Meg fold the very large, very bulky sweaters that her sturdily built mother had worn. Sweaters that Jenna—at five feet four inches, a hundred and ten pounds—would be lost in.

"Abby looks just like J.J. did as a baby, doesn't she?" Meg said then.

"*Just* like her," Jenna agreed, thinking about her late sister.

The initials stood for Joanna Janeane. An early-menopausal surprise for Jenna's parents, her sister had been named to appease both grandmothers after neither of them had been satisfied with the combination of their names that had produced Jenna's. Abby was the late J.J.'s fifteen-month-old daughter.

And at that moment the baby was napping in Jenna's room on the upper level of the old farmhouse that had now sheltered four generations of Bowens. Her grandfather had built the house and passed it down to her father, along with the small farm that had sustained the family until recent years.

Having both been twelve when J.J. was born, Jenna and Meg had done more than their fair share of babysitting for Jenna's much younger sibling, so it was easy to recall what she'd looked like and to see the resemblance now in her daughter.

"J.J. was a beautiful baby," Jenna added, fighting the grief that still rose at the memory of her sister.

"She was," Meg said in a commiserating tone.

"But so far, Abby doesn't seem quite as headstrong, and I'm grateful for that."

"Mmm," Meg agreed. "Although she might pick up a little of it from Tia because Tia has enough to share," Meg said with a laugh.

"Still, it'll be nice, raising little girls together," Jenna said. "I never thought we'd get to."

Certainly, unusual circumstances had made that come about. Marriage had made Meg stepmother to three-year-old Tia McKendrick. For Jenna, it was divorce and the loss of her younger sister, and then both of their parents, that had brought her back to her small Montana hometown of Northbridge, where she had just adopted her niece. In spite of the sadness and loss that had brought Jenna to that point, she was happy to be home again, to have Abby and to be in close proximity to Meg.

"Have you decided yet whether you're going to rent

an apartment on Main Street or take old Mrs. Wilkes's guesthouse—if we can't save this place?" Meg asked.

"It'll be the guesthouse," Jenna said. "It's tiny, but it has two bedrooms and a little bit of yard that Abby can go out into. And Mrs. Wilkes will give it to me dirt cheap in trade for some nursing—I'll look in on her every day, take her blood pressure, oversee her meds—"

"You'll work as a full-time nurse at the hospital and then go home to do more nursing?"

"I don't mind. Low rent will give me the chance to pay off some debt and save for a place of our own. Besides, Mrs. Wilkes loves Abby, and Abby loves her—I think maybe Mrs. Wilkes reminds Abby of Mom. It'll work out for everybody," Jenna finished, trying to sound upbeat.

But Meg knew her—and her situation—well enough to know how she really felt. "The fund *could* still get high enough for you to pay off the taxes or, at least, to put in a bid at the auction," Meg said, clearly attempting to inject some hope.

"It could," Jenna said without any more confidence than Meg had shown, smiling at her friend's weak optimism when they both knew neither of those possibilities was likely. Otherwise, they wouldn't be packing up.

The Bowen Farm Fund was an account initiated by an old friend of her father's. People could make donations to save the farm. There were several thousand dollars in it, but it was nowhere near forty thousand, and unless it reached the full amount of the tax debt, that money would be returned to the donors.

"Orrr..." Meg said.

"Nope," Jenna shot down what she knew her friend was going to say.

Meg said it anyway. "You could sell to the Kincaid Corporation and make enough money, even *after* paying off the back taxes, to buy a three-bedroom house right now."

Jenna shook her head. "I have enough to feel guilty about. I won't add not honoring my father's last wish to the list."

Meg didn't respond to that. Instead, glancing over Jenna's head in the direction of the living room as if something had caught her eye, she said, "Speak of the devil… Well, not that Ian Kincaid is the devil—he's actually really great."

Jenna swiveled on her rump until she had the same view Meg had.

Across the living room, through the nearly floor-to-ceiling picture window that looked out at the front porch, Jenna saw the local Realtor, Marsha Pinkell. And a man.

Oddly enough, it was the first time Jenna had seen Ian Kincaid.

Though he and his twin brother had been born in Northbridge, his connection to the small town was complicated. Ian was the biological brother of Chase Mackey, Meg's husband's business partner in Mackey and McKendrick Furniture Designs.

Over thirty years earlier, a car accident just outside of Northbridge had orphaned Chase, Shannon, twins Ian and Hutch, and a half sister. The half sister had gone to live with her birth father, Chase had ended up in the foster-care system, while Shannon had been adopted by one local couple, and the twin boys had been adopted by another, only to have both couples leave Northbridge almost immediately.

Only the half sister was old enough to remember she had brothers and a sister. Her desire to find a blood relative to raise her own child had prompted a search for the lost siblings and led her to Chase. Then, after Chase had located Shannon, together they'd discovered the whereabouts of Hutch and Ian.

Hutch had yet to appear, but Jenna had heard through Meg that Ian had been coming in and out of town since just after the first of the year to get to know Chase and Shannon.

Which was right about when Jenna's father had died and she'd had to put the farm up for sale, hoping to sell it before it was auctioned off by the IRS.

Since January, Ian Kincaid had also been to her farm several times with the Realtor to look at the place with an eye toward buying it. But Jenna had not been at home during any of his visits. Nor had her path crossed that of Ian Kincaid's in town.

Jenna had been swamped working long hours and caring for her father, then dealing with her father's death and the financial mess left in his wake. She'd also taken custody of Abby and was sorting through the legal issues of adopting her. Jenna had barely had time to come up for air.

Still, it seemed odd that Jenna had yet to encounter the man who had set all of Northbridge to talking—and arguing. The man who was interested in buying her farm. The man she wasn't interested in selling it to.

The man who now stood on her porch, six feet three

inches of athletic masculinity resembling Chase Mackey but taking Chase Mackey's size and increasing it slightly and improving upon Chase's noteworthy good looks while he was at it.

"Wow…" Jenna muttered involuntarily at that first glimpse of Ian Kincaid.

Meg laughed. "I know," she agreed, not requiring any explanation for the exclamation.

He was framed by the picture window but apparently looking at the structure of the house rather than through the plate glass into the interior, so he obviously had no idea he was being watched. And Jenna couldn't help watching—studying him, actually.

Slacks, a button-down shirt and a sports coat didn't hide the fact that the man was all broad shoulders, taut torso, narrow hips and long legs.

And above the broad shoulders?

There was no question that he was Chase Mackey's brother because the similarities were marked, particularly in the sexy dent in the center of his chin. But beyond that, Ian Kincaid's features took Chase's and refined them.

The lines of his face were more sharply defined, more angular. His jaw was chiseled. His nose was slightly longish but perfectly shaped. His lips had a hint more fullness to the lower than to the upper. His golden-brown, sun-kissed hair had the same waviness that Chase Mackey's had, but was cut shorter and neater all over. And his eyes…

Oh, those eyes!

Chase Mackey's were sky blue.

Ian Kincaid's were a more ethereal, almost translucent blue—like the sky reflected off a frozen pond.

"Wow…" Jenna heard herself say again as the full impact of those good looks sank in.

Meg laughed. "Uhh…Nurse Bowen? Should I throw cold water on you?"

"No… Right. He's the enemy," Jenna said to yank herself out of her reverie.

"Well, no, he isn't the devil or the enemy—he's a great guy—"

"Who could take over my dad's farm and turn it into a football training facility."

"You said you were coming to grips with that."

"I'm trying to." But she didn't need to be going gaga over the guy.

And yet, there she was, still staring at the man.

"Why don't we go out and I'll introduce you?" Meg suggested.

And why was concern for how she looked the first thing that flashed through Jenna's mind? Why should she care if her long, brown hair was still neatly in its ponytail or if the mascara had stayed on her brownish-green eyes? Why should she care that she had on baggy jeans and a too-big sweatshirt?

She shouldn't.

But she did.

"I'm a mess," she said, as if that were answer enough to Meg's suggestion.

"No, you're not. You look fine."

But somehow *fine* was not good enough when she thought of meeting the man who still had her staring.

"Come on," Meg urged. "Tia and Abby love him—"

"Abby knows him?"

"Well, sure. Even though you haven't met him, he's been around the showroom visiting his brother when I've babysat Abby."

Despite the fact that Meg babysat Abby whenever Jenna worked, and Ian Kincaid stayed in the above-the-garage apartment whenever he visited, Jenna hadn't met him.

"Tia and Abby both have the cutest little crushes on him," Meg continued. "Tia draws him scribbly pictures and bats her eyes at him and follows him around like a puppy dog if she can. And Abby holds out her arms for him to carry her the minute she sees him. She calls him *Un*, and out of the blue, she'll hug him and kiss him—it's so funny."

So his looks knocked the socks off little girls as well as big ones, Jenna thought. But what she said was, "Abby likes him?"

"She really does. And he's good with her, too. And with Tia. I know you don't like the idea that he wants the farm for something other than farming, but he really isn't a bad guy. You should meet him."

It didn't seem as if she was going to have a choice.

The Realtor glanced through the picture window and waved at Jenna and Meg. She said something to Ian Kincaid that made him look inside, too, and the two of them went to the front door and poked their heads in after an obligatory knock.

"Hi! I'm just showing Mr. Kincaid a few things he had questions about," Marsha Pinkell called. "Do you mind if we come in?"

The answer to that was yes, but that wasn't what Jenna

said. She could hardly refuse access to the Realtor she'd listed the farm with, so she said, "It's okay, come in."

They did just that as Jenna and Meg got up from the floor, so they could come face-to-face with Ian Kincaid.

"Hi, Ian," Meg greeted the man warmly.

"Hi, Meg," he answered with equal warmth and familiarity. "Logan said I might bump into you over here—I guess he was right."

"This is Jenna," Meg said. "Jenna Bowen. My best friend and Abby's aunt-slash-new-mom."

"And the owner of this place now—I know the name," Ian Kincaid added. "I also know that your father passed away not long ago. I'm sorry for your loss," he said, his eyes going from Meg to Jenna.

"Thank you," Jenna said perfunctorily, trying not to get too drawn into the not-at-all-cold gaze of those ice-blue eyes. They seemed to hone in on her. Again she wished for less baggy clothes, and that she'd done something different with her hair today.

"Marsha has also told me that—in honor of your dad—you're trying to hold tight to the contingent that this place continue as a working farm," he said.

"That's right," Jenna confirmed, seeing no reason to beat around the bush. "And I know that that isn't what you want to do with the place. That your father brought an NFL expansion football team to Montana and he wants to build a training center here."

"The Montana Monarchs," Ian Kincaid said the team's name as if she might not know it. "You're right on all counts. My father is Morgan Kincaid; he finally has his dream of owning an NFL team, and we need a training facility. We'll meet the asking price on the property without haggling if you'll just back off on that farm contingency."

"I won't. Not for any price. I realize if the place goes to auction, whoever buys it can do what they want with it. But as long as I still have the option, I'm holding to the contingency." Even if he was talking to her amiably, respectfully, pleasantly and as if they were on the same level when, in fact, she also knew that he was a bigwig in his former-football-star father's massive corporation and one of the heirs to a fortune, while she was merely a small-town nurse in debt.

"What if we sweeten the deal by, say, five thousand?" he said then.

"Doesn't that fall under the heading of haggling?" She goaded him just slightly.

To his credit, he smiled. A brilliant smile that exposed perfect white teeth and drew wonderful lines down the center of each cheek.

"I think haggling technically means I try to get you to lower the price, not that I offer you more money than you're asking," he countered.

"But I'm afraid it still falls under the 'not for any price' part," Jenna said, actually enjoying this exchange with him, the way she'd enjoyed debate team in high school.

"How about ten thousand?"

Jenna laughed, having no idea if he was serious. It didn't matter, but she liked the challenge he seemed to be throwing out.

She shook her head. "Not for any price," she repeated. "The farm has to be up for sale, but the contingency that it stay a farm isn't negotiable."

"I can be a pretty persuasive guy..."

She didn't doubt that! Not looking into those blue eyes that crinkled just a bit at the corners when he smiled and made her feel as if he didn't know there were two other people in the hallway with them.

"Persuasive or not, that's my sticking point," Jenna insisted.

"Hmm... Maybe I'll just have to try to figure out how to get you unstuck..."

"Good luck with that," she said as if she were impervious to anything he might come up with. Even to the hint of flirting in his voice.

He laughed. Not boisterously, but a small, light laugh that almost seemed if they'd shared a private joke. And again, Jenna couldn't help being a bit drawn in by the man.

But maybe that was how he got what he wanted, she told herself, unwilling to think that sparks might actually be flying between them—which was the way it somehow felt.

His gaze remained on her a moment more before he angled his head in the direction of the closet. "We should let you and Meg get back to what you were doing," he said then.

"Yeah, I won't have her help for much longer this afternoon, and I want to get as much work out of her as I can," Jenna joked.

"It was good to finally meet you, though, Jenna Bowen," Ian Kincaid said as if he meant it.

"You, too," Jenna responded.

And while she'd intended that to be only as perfunctory as her gratitude for his condolences had been, it had somehow come out as more than that. As genuine.

Good to meet the man who would very likely be instrumental in dashing her late father's one wish?

She wasn't sure how that could be.

And yet the truth was that as he said goodbye to Meg, as Jenna watched him turn and walk out her front door with the Realtor, she was a little sorry to see him go.

"Didn't I tell you?" Meg whispered from beside her. "He's nice, isn't he?"

"Nice to look at," was all Jenna would admit to as she drank in the sight of the tall, straight-backed, commanding man going outside again.

But whether she admitted it or not, there hadn't been anything unlikeable about Ian Kincaid.

In fact, a little part of her that she didn't want to acknowledge had liked him quite a bit…

Chapter Two

Sunday was unseasonably warm for early spring, and Ian decided to take advantage of it and go out to the Bowen property without the Realtor.

The farm wasn't far from the Mackey and McKendrick compound where he was staying, where he'd stayed on all the occasions he'd come to Northbridge since his long lost brother and sister had contacted him at Christmas. In fact, the Bowen place was almost next door. But he wasn't going from the compound to the farm.

He was headed out to the Bowen place from Northbridge proper after attending a church pancake breakfast with his brother Chase, Chase's wife, Hadley, and seventeen-month-old Cody—the nephew who had reunited Ian, Chase and Shannon. The nephew Chase was raising.

Shannon and her soon-to-be husband, Dag McKendrick,

had also been there, so the town event had turned into a family breakfast for Ian, which was part of why he liked coming to Northbridge now.

The family component was also part of why he'd chosen the small town as the site for the training center for the Montana Monarchs football team.

He'd known that Northbridge existed, that it was where he and Hutch had been born, where their birth parents had died, where he and Hutch had been adopted. But he and Hutch had been barely two months old when that adoption had occurred and they'd been taken away from Northbridge. Since they'd never returned, Northbridge had been nothing but a name on a map.

Then Ian had received an email from Chase and Shannon telling him that Hutch wasn't his only sibling. He'd reconnected with the small town in the course of reconnecting with his brother and sister.

Not that it wasn't the perfect place for the training center, because it was. It was far enough from Billings to reduce distractions, but close enough to make it easy for the players, the staff, the coaches and trainers and the press to get to. It also didn't make for a bad drive for visits from families left behind in Billings.

And Ian liked the idea that, as Chief Operating Officer for the Monarchs, he would spend plenty of time in Northbridge where Chase, Shannon and Cody lived.

After a rift had healed between Ian and his adoptive father, they were once again close. He was also close to his adoptive sister Lacey. But he and his twin brother Hutch? That was a different story. They hadn't seen each other or spoken in over five—almost six—years.

Maybe that was why developing closer relationships

with his newfound blood relatives was all the more important to him, and it *was* important to him. Bringing the training center to Northbridge would aid that cause.

He had his father onboard with Northbridge, so that wasn't a problem. And there were two possible sites within the Northbridge area—the Bowen farm and another, slightly larger location several miles farther out of town.

But of the two, the Bowen place was the most ideal. At seventeen acres it was a better size than its twenty-four acre contender which would leave excess acreage. It also lacked the large hill the McDoogal property had that would have to be leveled to accommodate playing fields. Plus, even if Jenna Bowen took him up on the extra ten thousand dollars he'd sweetened the pot with yesterday, the price on the Bowen place was still far better—it was priced low in hopes of a fast sale.

But Jenna Bowen was holding out, trying to keep the place a working farm, even in the face of an enormous debt in unpaid taxes. It was that enormous debt that had the property scheduled to be auctioned off in ten days if she couldn't raise the money before then.

What that meant to the Kincaid Corporation was that they could get the property one way or another. If it went to auction, the Kincaid Corporation would likely end up getting it for a song, in fact. But buying the place at auction wasn't really the image the Kincaid Corporation or the Monarchs wanted to foster. Even if it did save some money.

About half of Northbridge was against bringing the training camp to the small town, against losing farmland to it, and certainly against one of their own family farms being bulldozed by a corporation that, if they bought at auction, would ultimately end up seeming to be on the side of the IRS. That same half wanted to help the Bowens keep the property long enough to sell to someone who would honor their wishes for the land.

So ultimately, Ian had two factions to win over to his side—that half of the town. And Jenna Bowen.

He was up for it, though. He was even looking forward to it.

Convincing half of Northbridge that it was a good idea to bring the training center in would be a challenge, but that was okay. He liked challenges. And when he showed people that he did business with honesty, integrity and straightforwardness, when he pointed out the positives, he felt certain he'd be able to rally even the unenthusiastic portion of Northbridge.

But Jenna Bowen?

She was a different story. She obviously had an emotional involvement that would take more finesse, more personal attention to conquer—if it could be conquered at all. And to that end, he'd decided it was time they met. That had been the purpose of having the Realtor take him out to her farm yesterday, when he'd known that she would be there because he'd overheard Meg tell Logan that she and Jenna would be packing up the household.

That hadn't been the first time he'd seen her, though.

When he stayed at the compound he used a small studio apartment above the detached garage behind the main house. From that vantage point, he'd had an occasional sighting of Jenna Bowen over the months when Meg had provided babysitting for Abby, and Jenna had come to drop off or pick up the baby.

No, they hadn't had the opportunity to meet—that just hadn't worked out until yesterday. But it had given him the chance to do some preliminary study of Meg's best friend.

Jenna Bowen was a small-town beauty, he thought as he drove out of Northbridge to get to the farm and the picture of her popped into his head.

Actually, she could hold her own with most big-city beauties, too, he'd decided when he'd finally had his first close-up view of her at her house on Saturday.

No, she wasn't high-fashion-model material, like Chelsea Tanner—the woman his father was itching for him to marry. But Jenna Bowen was definitely no slouch in the looks department.

Hers wasn't an aloof, cutting-edge sort of beauty, the way Chelsea's was. Instead there was a warmth, a sweetness to Jenna Bowen's appearance. A naturalness. Something that had made it difficult for him to ultimately take his eyes off of…

She had skin like peaches and cream—flawless, smooth and so soft-looking he'd had the urge to reach out and run the backs of his fingers along one cheek to see if it could possibly feel the way it appeared.

Her hair was long and wavy, a glistening brown. In his isolated glimpses of her, he'd seen it pulled back, he'd seen it tied up, he'd seen it the way he liked it best—falling full and free around her face to at least four inches below her shoulders, like a shining, vibrant cascade of cocoa.

And her eyes…

Ah, her eyes…

Those distant sightings had kept him in the dark about

her eyes but on yesterday's visit to the farm he'd finally been able to see them for himself. To see her long, thick lashes dusting eyes that were a similar brown to her hair except that they weren't completely brown.

No, her eyes had some green in them—a glimmering green, like secret, hidden emeralds—making them interesting, intriguing, stunning.

Her nose was thin and not terribly long. She had petal-pink lips, perfect white teeth and high, apple-bright cheeks that gave her some of that country appeal, too.

Her neck was long and a little thin, and she had such perfect posture that it made her fairly short stature—five three or four, maybe—seem like more.

And the body that went with it all?

Compact but still curvaceous enough to have had him wondering how she would look without clothes…

Not that he had any business doing *that!*

Work, the training facility, Chelsea Tanner and getting Tanner Brewery to sponsor the Monarchs—that was what he was supposed to be focused on now, he reminded himself as he neared the Bowen farm. Chelsea Tanner, whom his father would be thrilled to have him hook up with. Chelsea Tanner, whom his father believed would be a great match for him and for the future connection between the Montana Monarchs and Chelsea Tanner's father's brewery dollars.

The trouble was, Chelsea Tanner just didn't do it for him. They'd met at the huge party his father had thrown when Morgan had been granted the NFL franchise. They'd hit it off. But merely as friends. The fact that it could be a match made in business heaven? That was all his father could see. But for Ian? A beautiful face, long legs and a shared interest in Jazz weren't enough.

In his mind's eye, the image of Jenna Bowen was edging out that of the supermodel….

But he was getting the shove from Chelsea's father, too.

Chelsea's father wanted Ian to lure Chelsea back from one of her many photo shoots in Europe in the hopes that she might be interested in becoming the spokesmodel for Tanner Brewery in order to add a little class. And to keep his daughter closer to home.

Ian was working on convincing Chelsea to come home and become the face of Tanner Brewery. But beyond that? Sharing their jazz playlists was the only other thing he was interested in. The only thing Chelsea was interested in with him, too.

Ian turned off the main road onto the path that led to the Bowen property's boundary.

Hardly a road, it was pitted and bumpy. It was difficult to decide which of the tractor-tire ruts he should stick to. It was definitely more rustic than the paved drive, with its white rail fence on either side, that led to the house. But he wanted a view of the place from one of its edges so he could look out over the whole seventeen acres and get a clear picture in his mind about the best layout for the center. So, the dirt road it was.

He didn't go any farther than he had to, however, before he pulled to a stop.

Then, with the engine still running, he put the car into park, grabbed the binoculars he'd brought with him for this purpose and got out.

No doubt about it—this was the perfect location for

the training facility, he thought, as he looked out over the property through the binoculars. Flat farmland, wide, open space except for the small barn and the house that would be leveled in favor of the administrative building that would be the entrance to the center.

But when Jenna emerged from the back door carrying baby Abby, it was the existing house that held his interest.

Ian had the impression that Jenna was taking advantage of the weather, too. She didn't seem to have any real reason to be outside, and she was clearly dressed for work, since she was wearing dark purple scrubs. But still, she carried Abby into the yard and pointed to a bird sitting on a post of the paddock fence as she said something to the infant.

Abby was a sweet baby. And as cute as they came, with her honey-blond, curly cap of hair, her chubby cheeks and her big, brown eyes.

And Jenna was her aunt-slash-new-mom….

Ian recalled how Meg had introduced her friend, and it didn't make sense to him. He had just assumed that Abby was Jenna's daughter, plain and simple. But that didn't seem to be the case. As he watched the two now, he didn't see anything that would indicate that Jenna wasn't Abby's mother, however.

Abby was yet another reason he needed not to go off on flights of fancy over Jenna Bowen. He liked Abby, but he was at least ten years from wanting kids in his own life. And when that happened, they had to be his biological kids.

That was *his* sticking point.

Just as he was thinking that—and still watching Jenna

and Abby through the binoculars—he saw Jenna lightly kiss Abby's cheek.

Then, as if the gesture hadn't been done right, Abby grabbed both sides of Jenna's face in her two pudgy little hands and gave her a return kiss that had a whole lot more oomph to it.

The scene made Ian laugh at the same time Jenna did, just before she twirled around with the infant, making Abby laugh along with her.

And out of the blue—for absolutely no reason Ian could put his finger on—he felt like he should drive over there and say hello.

That was a little strange—the sudden yen to be a part of what he was spying on.

Of course, it *was* a great day in the country, he did get a kick out of Abby, and Jenna was a naturally beautiful, fresh-faced woman whom he'd enjoyed talking to for that brief time yesterday. So maybe it wasn't really such a big mystery that he felt like saying hello.

Well, the mystery might be in the intensity he was feeling to get to them, but still he reasoned that he did need to be establishing a relationship with Jenna Bowen. So why not take advantage of the day, the situation, the coincidence and the convenience of having her right there, no more than a two-minute drive around a U-shaped dirt path?

He'd be silly *not* to take advantage of all that and lay some groundwork for a purely friendly relationship with her that could potentially benefit them both, wouldn't he?

Sure he would.

Now he just needed to take his eyes off of her to do that....

He forced himself to lower the binoculars, to get back in the car, feeling oddly grateful that the engine was still running, and that all he had to do was put it into gear.

And if he was in such a hurry to get to her that he left huge plumes of dust behind him when he hit the gas?

It didn't mean anything.

And neither did his lack of concern for how bumpy a ride it was on that road or what it was doing to his shocks not to take any care with how he drove.

He was merely going to extend a simple greeting to the farm owner he would like to convince to do business with him.

And the fact that the farm owner was the lovely-to-look-at Jenna Bowen meant nothing at all...

As Montana winters went weather-wise, Jenna's first one back hadn't been particularly bad. But since she'd lost both of her parents during that period of time, it had felt very bleak. So that first, early taste of spring on Sunday was a welcome relief.

She had to be at the hospital for a three-to-eleven shift but—not wanting to waste the warmth and sunshine—she'd decided to take Abby outside for a little while.

She hadn't been out the back door for more than a few minutes when the sudden stirring of dust over on the border road drew her attention.

"Looks like we're gonna have company," she told Abby, inching back in the direction of the house.

During the last ten years, she'd lived in several places where being cautious was advisable, and while she might be back in Northbridge, she still didn't recognize the expensive black import that was coming her way. Just in case her drop-in visitor wasn't welcome, she wanted the ability to duck inside in a hurry.

In fact, she was standing so that she and Abby were in the lee of the screen door, where one step would take them over the threshold to safety, when the car drew near enough for her to see that it was Ian Kincaid behind the wheel.

*Of course...*Jenna thought as a completely inexplicable sense of excitement replaced her trepidation.

He drove around the side of the house before he came to a stop. Jenna heard him turn off the engine and get out, shutting the door after himself.

Then he appeared around the corner.

"Hi," he called, tossing her a smile that she liked more than she had any reason to.

"Hello," Jenna said, keeping it somewhat formal, despite her reactions to the man. Or maybe to hide those reactions....

"It was such a nice day I wanted to come out and look around a little more." He pointed in the direction he'd come from. "I was on that other road when I saw you. I thought maybe I should drop over and make sure you don't mind. If you do, I'll take off." He finished with a gesture of surrender that raised his hands to the height of his extremely broad shoulders.

His big, strong-looking hands that Jenna couldn't help noticing right along with the shoulders. He wore brown tweed slacks and a tan shirt that made him look too dressed up for a lazy, Sunday afternoon in Northbridge, but impressively good nonetheless.

"Un!" Abby said then, bending far away from Jenna and putting her arms out to Ian as he drew near.

"Hi, Abby," he said to the infant with an even warmer smile. Then to Jenna he added, "That's what she calls me—'Un.' Abby and I are old friends."

"So Meg said."

"Can I take her?" he asked.

Since Abby wasn't giving her much choice, and Jenna knew that Meg had come to trust him around both Abby and Tia, Jenna abandoned the doorway and handed over the infant.

Abby promptly curved one arm around the back of Ian's muscular neck as if she belonged there and was staking her claim on him.

"Meg told me you've made quite an impression on both Abby and Tia," Jenna said.

"I'd like to say all the girls love me, but I'm pretty sure you could refute that, so I won't," he joked.

He did seem like kind of a hard person to *dis*like, but Jenna kept that to herself. Instead she said, "It's been a rotten winter for me, and I have spring fever something fierce today so, even though it's a little early for it, I made fresh lemonade. Would you like a glass?"

"Sounds great. But why don't we sit on your porch to drink it so you can still get some of this nice weather? I'll take Abby around to the front, and you can meet us there."

Was he thoughtful or good at orchestrating things or giving orders? Jenna wasn't sure. But the idea of a glass of lemonade on the front porch—okay, yes, *with him*—was too appealing for her to balk at, one way or another, so she said, "Okay."

As she went inside, put ice in two tall glasses and poured their drinks, Jenna hoped that Ian Kincaid wasn't there to try to talk her into selling the farm to him. It was such a nice day, she wanted to enjoy it, and that was a subject that would ruin it.

Maybe, if he did bring it up, a firm no coupled with an "I don't want to talk about it," would stop him.

If not, she might take Abby and her lemonade and just go inside, because she was not going to let him put a damper on today.

As Jenna carried the glasses down the hallway to the front door she'd opened earlier to let in some fresh air, she could see Abby and Ian Kincaid through the screen. It gave her a clue as to one of the reasons Abby liked him. He was sitting on the porch floor at the top of the stairs. The little girl straddled his ankle while he held both of her hands and bounced her up and down with the rise and fall of that long leg.

Jenna knew from doing that herself that Abby adored what Jenna called a horsey-ride, and the baby's giggling delight only confirmed it.

"Mo!" Abby demanded when Ian paused to glance over his shoulder at the sound of Jenna coming out onto the porch.

"That's Abby-speak for more," Jenna informed him. "And the problem with horsey-ride is that she never wants you to stop."

"Yeah, I've learned that," he said. Then, to Abby he called an enthusiastic, "Here comes the big finish!"

As Jenna crossed the wide wrap-around porch to join them, Ian gave Abby a wild enough ride to make the infant squeal before he slowed by increments and made winding-down noises.

To Jenna's surprise, when he finally stopped altogether and hoisted Abby to his lap, the little girl accepted it without further complaint.

"So that's the secret?" Jenna observed. "I have to say 'here comes the big finish,' give her a grand finale and some sound effects, and she lets it end?"

"That's my trick. I don't know if it'll work for you," he said, settling Abby in the crook of one arm so he could take the glass of lemonade that Jenna offered.

Once he had, she sat beside him, making sure she left all the space that could be left between them in what was allotted by the porch railing.

She set her own glass of lemonade down and held out her arms to Abby. "Why don't you come and sit with me now and have some lemonade?"

"No," Abby answered, pushing back into the arm that provided a sturdy support for her back.

"Oh, she *does* like you," Jenna said, showing a hint of the rejection she felt.

Ian merely grinned and sipped his lemonade. Letting the comment pass, he said, "As Montana winters go, this last one was pretty mild. Why was it rotten for you?"

He'd paid attention to what she'd said earlier....

"I came back to Northbridge in October when my mother died suddenly of a heart attack during a blizzard. That trip was when I first realized my dad's emphysema was much, much worse than I'd been told. I decided to stay to take care of him, but we still lost him the first week of January. Which was about the time I also found out about the tax debt—"

"Ah, it wasn't so much the weather as what happened this winter. And that was a lot," he agreed. "I didn't know you'd lost your mother right before your father. I lost my mother when I was eleven and that was bad enough. Losing both of your parents within months of each other must have been doubly rough."

Made rougher by the guilt she carried, but she didn't offer that information. "It was."

"You said you came back when your mom passed away?" he said then. "Does that mean that you weren't living in Northbridge?"

"Not at the time, no. I wanted to be, but that hadn't worked out yet. It sort of had to in a hurry after I saw that my dad was failing. Plus there was Abby…"

Abby, whom she didn't really want to share, so Jenna again held out her hands to the baby.

Who once more chose to remain with Ian.

Abby did take the drink of Jenna's lemonade that Jenna offered, though.

"Tell me about Miss Abby here," Ian said then. "Meg introduced you as her aunt-slash-new-mom—what exactly does that mean?"

"She's my niece and now my adopted daughter, too," Jenna answered as if it were simple.

"So you have a brother or a sister?" he said, sorting through it.

"I did have a sister. We called her J.J. She was twelve years younger than me, and only sixteen when she got pregnant and had Abby—"

"Oh," Ian said, as if that explanation left him with more questions.

Anticipating them, Jenna said, "My folks talked J.J. into keeping Abby by promising to help raise her—"

"The dad wasn't in the picture?"

"The dad was one of the boys at the school for troubled and delinquent kids just outside of town. Unfortunately, he was still in the picture, but since he had no family at all, it was still really up to Mom and Dad—"

"And sixteen-year-old J.J."

"Right. Until J.J. and Abby's dad went joyriding when Abby was four months old..." Jenna swallowed back the lump that instantly formed in her throat. "Both J.J. and Abby's dad were killed when the car hit a pothole and rolled over. Then it was just up to Mom and Dad."

"Who weren't in good health," Ian added.

"At the time no one knew my mom had anything going on with her heart—no one knew until the attack that killed her. My dad's emphysema was slowing him down then, but he was still working the farm, so they didn't really think their health was an issue. I talked about taking Abby, but my own situation was...difficult, so Mom and Dad just kept the status quo—they'd been doing the lion's share of taking care of Abby, they said they could just go on taking care of her."

"But then in a snap they were both gone...."

"Right. And then there was just Abby and me. And my situation had changed—" Jenna leaned forward enough to tickle Abby's rib cage "—and I wanted this little stinker, so I adopted her."

"Which makes you her aunt and her mom now."

"Right," Jenna said in a positive tone to let him know how happy she was to find herself Abby's mother. "Of course, I'll let her know about J.J. and her dad, but I'll really just be Mom—which I'm working on getting her to call me."

As if to show her willingness to accept Jenna in that role, Abby finally held out her arms for Jenna to take her.

Ian set his nearly empty glass of lemonade on the porch and freed the way for Jenna to reach for the infant.

To do that, Jenna had to slip one of her hands between Abby's side and Ian's front. There was no avoiding making contact with him.

What Jenna should have been able to avoid was being as aware as she was of the hard wall of muscles she felt behind his shirt. And liking the way it felt against the back of her hand…

You're a nurse, for crying out loud! You make physical contact with people for a living! she silently chastised herself to battle the tingling that that particular contact had set off along the surface of her skin.

Gratefully, Ian Kincaid didn't seem to know she was having that response to him as she lifted Abby from his lap to Jenna's and became very intent on giving her niece more lemonade.

"I should probably go—I saw what I came to see and I'm figuring from the scrubs that you must have to get to work at some point," Ian said then—in a voice that seemed slightly lower than it had been and suddenly made Jenna worry that he did know something was happening with her.

But even if that was true, he, too, found refuge in Abby by fiddling with one of her curls when he said, "Bye, Abby."

"Bye," Abby answered perfunctorily, waving a

chubby hand to go along with it, the way she'd been tutored.

Then, to Jenna, Ian said, "Thanks for the lemonade. This was nice."

"Sure," was all she said as she watched him get to his feet.

He paused a moment, and she couldn't tell what was going through his mind before he said, "Tomorrow night is the grand opening of Mackey and McKendrick Furniture Designs—will you be there?"

"I will be," she said.

A slow smile spread across his handsome face. "Good…I'm glad…." He answered almost as if he shouldn't be admitting it.

Then he headed for his car, and Jenna watched him go.

And watched him and watched him, drinking in every last drop of the sight of the best derriere she thought she'd ever seen.

Until he rounded the side of the house, and she couldn't see him anymore.

And she was a little sorry about that…

So apparently, he hadn't put a damper on her day.

But as for the rest—the skin-tingling on contact, the ogling of his backside when he'd walked away, the fact that she'd enjoyed spending that brief time with him?

She didn't know where any of that had come from.

But she did know that there was no place in her life for it.

Not now. Not with him.

In the last eleven months, she'd gone from one disaster to another. The death of J.J. and of Abby's dad. Her own divorce. Her mother's death. Her father's. The tax debacle and the likelihood that she was going to lose the farm. She'd gone from chaos to more chaos to even more chaos.

And it had to end. For both her own sake and for Abby's. They needed to find a little solace, a little calm, a little peace. To settle down, to settle in. Together. Just the two of them.

Nowhere in any of that was there a place for skin-tingling or ogling or enjoying Ian Kincaid's company.

In fact, a man—any man—but certainly Ian Kincaid of all men, was the anti-solace, the anti-calm, the anti-peace, the anti-settling down, the anti-settling in.

And Jenna wasn't having any part of that.

So why was she suddenly looking forward to tomorrow night's grand opening of Mackey and McKendrick Furniture Designs even more than she had been?

It didn't matter why.

She just knew she needed to squash it.

And that was what she was determined to do.

Although that little bit of a thrill at the thought that Ian Kincaid would be there was hard to catch and squash when it again took flight at merely the glimpse of him behind the wheel of his car as he drove from the side of her house and waved on his way to the main road.

But still she was determined.

Peace and calm and solace, settling in, settling down—that was what she was going to find, to achieve, for herself and for Abby.

Without the disruption of a guy who made her skin tingle…

Chapter Three

"What do you think, Abby? Too much?" Jenna asked her niece as she stood in front of the full-length mirror early Monday evening.

Of course, Abby didn't respond. The fifteen-month-old was occupied with the bottom drawer of Jenna's dresser, exploring and dragging out every scarf, glove and whatnot she found there.

After feeding Abby dinner, Jenna had taken the baby upstairs with her and set her in the crib with a slew of toys to keep her safely entertained so Jenna could take a quick shower and shampoo her hair.

Then she'd retrieved Abby and brought the little girl with her to her bedroom, where she'd set Abby on the floor. Being let loose in Jenna's room always meant one of two things for the infant—either she played in the closet or she opened the bottom dresser drawer. Since Jenna had had problems picking out what to wear tonight, Abby had already demolished the closet and moved on to the drawer.

But Jenna was intent on looking her best for the grand opening of Mackey and McKendrick Furniture Designs.

The cocktail affair was to be casual, but somehow Jenna didn't want to go *too* casual. So while she'd opted for jeans, they were her dressiest jeans—jeans she'd paid a small fortune for because they rode every curve to perfection and managed to transform her rear end into a much better shape than she thought it had on its own.

To go along with the jeans, she was wearing a black, crocheted-lace blouse over a strapless black, spandex tube top. And for shoes she was trying on her post-divorce-first-night-on-the-town-with-the-girls-to-prove-she-could-still-get-hit-on shoes—peekaboo-toed, black patent leathers with bows and four-inch heels.

And she *had* gotten hit on that night. In those shoes. And that same outfit….

Not that she was aiming to get hit on tonight, of course. She wasn't. She just wanted to look good. This was really the first fancy evening social event she'd gone to since being back in Northbridge.

And the fact that Ian Kincaid was going to be there? That he'd made a point of asking if she was going to be there, too?

Okay, maybe that had a teensy, weensy bit to do with the fact that she wanted to look good. But that was all. And it was just a matter of pride. Yes, her father had died owing the government over forty-thousand dollars in unpaid taxes that she couldn't pay, either; yes, Ian Kincaid and the Kincaid Corporation might be able to get her father's farm and turn it into a football training center, whether she liked it or not, but she still had her dignity. And that outfit and those shoes.

And maybe tonight she wanted to think that she might be able to make Ian Kincaid eat his heart out just a little…

"As if that could happen," she told her reflection in the mirror, to bring herself back down to earth.

After all, she reasoned as she applied some blush, some eye shadow, some mascara, she was thirty not twenty—if she were still twenty, she wouldn't have even needed the blush. She was a nurse, not a doctor—the way she'd set out to be. She was divorced after ten years of marriage to a man whose mother had been and still was more important than Jenna had ever managed to be to him. And while a lot of her male patients flirted shamelessly with her, most of them were elderly.

Second looks from guys her own age? Sure, those she got now and then. But despite the fact that following Ted to Mexico and then to several states in his failed career pursuits had made her fairly well-traveled, she'd never acquired any sort of sophistication. She was still a small-town girl through and through. And it was there on the girl-next-door face that she didn't have complaints about, but that didn't make men like Ian Kincaid drool, so there was no reason to think that he was going to.

And even if he did, so what? she asked herself as she bent over to give her hair a thorough brushing before standing straight again to fluff it and let it fall in loose waves around her shoulders.

Besides being desperate to find some serenity in her life, she was fresh out of a marriage that had completely revolved around her former husband and his—well, actually, his mother's—goals for him. For Ted and his mother, she'd sacrificed everything—including her own dreams and having kids and time she should have spent with her family.

If she hadn't, her family might not have ended up the way it had.

And while she didn't know much about Ian, she did know that he worked for his father. To her, that meant that meeting his boss's requirements wasn't something he could leave at the office. It meant that his father held two major positions of importance in his life, and that gave his father double the power over him, double the influence over him, double the reason for Ian to factor in his father's opinions, desires and goals, and try to please him above and before all else. Above and before everyone else.

For Jenna, that raised red warning flares.

In her experience, a family tie that strong ended up taking the number one priority.

And getting lost in the dust of accommodating that wasn't something she was ever—*ever*—going to do again. The cost was just too high.

"So we don't care whether or not Ian Kincaid's jaw drops tonight," she muttered to Abby, who was trying to pull a stocking cap over her own curly hair and again paid Jenna no attention.

But still it would be a really nice ego-boost if his jaw did drop, she couldn't help thinking.

And it certainly wouldn't hurt to have a bit of an ego boost after this winter.

It just wouldn't change anything, Jenna swore.

She had set a new course for herself, for her life. An unwavering course.

Ian Kincaid might be drop-dead gorgeous, a pleasure to sit on the porch and drink lemonade with, sexy enough to have had her fantasizing about him all through the night, on her mind this entire day—or not—but he was also a guy to stay away from, even if she *wasn't* intent on sticking to her own new path.

So an ego boost was honestly all she wanted from him. All she would allow.

But if his jaw dropped when she walked in tonight?

She'd be glad for that ego boost.

Then she'd go on about her business and never give him another thought.

The grand opening of Mackey and McKendrick Furniture Designs was by invitation only; Jenna had helped Meg address them and knew that over two hundred of them had gone out.

The main house on the compound—the house Meg shared with her husband Logan and Tia—was being used as the babysitting center. Manned by four teenage girls, that was where Meg's three-year-old stepdaughter and several other children and infants were being left.

Abby was not altogether good with strangers and clung to Jenna when the babysitters tried to take her, but after a moment of watching Tia—whom Abby treated like a big sister—Abby motioned to be let down. She crawled over to where the three-year-old was playing. Since Tia welcomed Abby and let her play with the train set, too, Jenna felt free to leave her and went through the house and out the back door.

Directly behind Meg's home was a large two-car garage. Over that was the studio apartment where Jenna knew Ian was staying. There weren't any lights on there, so she assumed he was already at the party.

A shiver of excitement ran through her at that thought, the thought that she was on her way to seeing him again.

Then she got furious at herself.

She was also on her way to seeing potentially two hundred other people, she reminded herself. Why was it only Ian Kincaid she was thinking about and getting excited over?

Take it down a notch, she warned herself.

But still she walked a little faster to get to the party.

It was being held next door to the garage, in what had once been the property's barn. The top half had been converted into a loft where Chase Mackey lived with his soon-to-be-wife, Hadley, and Ian and Chase's nephew, Cody.

The lower half of the barn was devoted to Mackey and McKendrick Furniture Designs. The rear portion was work space, while the front half had been turned into showcases that displayed the furniture to best effect. Those showcases had taken from December until now to finally complete.

As Jenna neared the big barn doors that were open for the event, she could see light spilling out and hear the sounds of the guitarist and singer Meg had hired, as well as laughter and many, many voices.

As hosts and hostesses, Meg, Logan, Chase and Hadley were positioned at the entrance to greet new arrivals. The mayor and his wife were taking up their attention as Jenna got there, so she motioned to Meg to let her know she was just going to go in, and then she moved around them, headed for the sea of people.

She spotted several of the Perrys and the Pratts she'd grown up with, and she took a moment to chat with them. She said hello to the Graysons, who were new to town but whom Meg had introduced her to. Logan and Hadley's half siblings were there—although Jenna didn't see Dag and his new wife Shannon, Ian's sister. All of the other business owners in town were there, along with the entire town council and even a few people who looked familiar, but whom Jenna couldn't quite place.

The one person she didn't see was Ian Kincaid.

Not that it made any difference, she told herself. She knew almost everyone there, she was looking forward to talking to many people she hadn't yet had the chance to reconnect with, and it didn't make any difference if she never encountered him tonight.

Except that somehow in her scenario of making her entrance, she'd imagined him alone in the distance when he caught his first sight of her and being bowled over by it.

Silly. It was just so silly....

When it struck her just how silly it was, she shuddered a little at having had such an adolescent pipe dream and vowed to put Ian Kincaid completely from her mind. This was a party she'd been looking forward to before she'd even met him, and she was determined to dive into it, to enjoy herself and not to have another thought about the man.

Starting now!

Since Logan, Chase and Hadley—who worked with Logan and Chase as their upholsterer—had been busy decorating the showcases, Meg had taken charge of the party planning, and Jenna had helped her friend wherever she could. Part of that help had involved deciding where to put the bar, the hors d'oeuvres table and the guitarist and singer. So even though she couldn't see any of those things through the crowd, she knew what direction to go to get to them.

It took time to move through the mass of people, because she *did* know most everyone, and there were so many more greetings to exchange along the way.

Then she finally made it to her destination, and that was where she found Ian Kincaid.

He was standing alone near the bar, rather than in the middle of the showroom floor, and his jaw didn't drop when he first caught sight of Jenna. But his striking pale blue eyes did widen, and that supple-looking mouth of his stretched into a slow, appreciative smile that still managed to send the message she'd been hoping for.

"This is not the look of a farmer's daughter," he said when Jenna reached the bar and he stepped up to meet her as if he'd been waiting for her.

"What are farmers' daughters supposed to look like?" Jenna asked, raising her chin in challenge and suppressing a smile of her own.

"Not as good as you look," he said, tilting his head to take in the full view now that he was nearer.

And while Jenna lectured herself about how it shouldn't please her to have his reaction be what she'd hoped for, it still thrilled her to no end.

"Can I buy you a drink?" he asked then.

"It's an open bar," Jenna pointed out.

His smile turned into a mischievous half grin that told her he'd known that all along.

"I'll have a glass of red wine," she told the bartender, bypassing Ian.

"Make it two," he added over his shoulder as he leaned an elbow on the bar and focused his attention solely on Jenna.

Despite that, just as the bartender poured their wine and slid the glasses to them, three old friends came up to say hello to Jenna and put in drink orders of their own.

As Jenna chatted with them, Ian stayed where he was. It seemed rude of her not to introduce him, so she did.

"Are you here together?" Neily Pratt—one of the three old friends—asked Jenna.

"No!" Jenna answered much too quickly.

Ian chuckled quietly, as if her discomfort at that question amused him.

"But you were talking when we came up, so we'll leave you alone," Neily added when the other three glasses of wine had been delivered.

"Would it be so bad if we were together?" Ian asked when the women had moved off. "Because Shannon isn't here yet, and everybody else I know is busy. I was hoping you'd have pity on me and keep me company."

"Out of pity?" she repeated, teasing him with the word.

"I'll take what I can get," he joked back, as if he were desperate.

Being in a large group and not knowing anyone was something Jenna was far more familiar with than she wished she was. Too many moves to too many cities as Ted attempted to find a medical specialty he could tolerate had required her getting too many new jobs, frequently putting her in that position. And each and every time it had happened she'd hated it so much that she did feel a little sorry for Ian, the fish out of water in this gathering of Northbridge townsfolk.

Or at least that was what she told herself when, rather than abandoning him, she said, "We should at least move, we're right in the way of everyone getting drinks."

Which was true enough as several more people gathered there.

"Come on, I'll show you my favorite showcase," Ian urged.

Curious about his taste, Jenna agreed. What she hadn't expected was for him to take her elbow to guide her to the very back of the showroom portion of the remodeled barn. Or to have that hand at her elbow feel warm and strong and much, much better than it had any reason to feel.

In fact it felt so good that she lost track of everything around her and only regained her wits when she found herself in the display right next to the door to the work room.

Almost no one was venturing back that far, and it was a distance from the music as well, so it was fairly quiet. They were now in the business–office showcase that displayed bookcases and filing cabinets positioned around an enormous desk that was the centerpiece.

"You can help me guard this so no one comes back here and scratches it or puts a wet glass on it—I just bought it, so it's mine."

He gestured at the desk. The base was antiqued black,

and the top was walnut with a subtle carving along the edges to soften the line.

"It's a beautiful desk," Jenna said, studying the piece of furniture as he turned to lean against it like a sentry.

"Handmade by Chase," Ian informed her. "Not only did I like it, but I like the idea of having something he designed, crafted and carved himself."

"That's really nice," Jenna said, meaning it. It moved her that he was trying to forge bonds between himself and his newly discovered family.

Then, without intending it, her gaze went from the desk to him.

He looked amazing in a pair of pin-striped gray wool slacks and a charcoal-colored mock-neck sweater that she had no doubt was cashmere. Too amazing—she was a little afraid of her own jaw dropping.

So she followed his lead, turned around and leaned on the desk much the way he was, making sure to keep a respectable distance between his hips and her own.

With both of them facing the mingling crowd of people beyond the showcase, Ian nodded his chin at them and said, "So do you know everybody?"

"Pretty much—I did grow up here."

"Along with Chase, Logan and Hadley—they've told me stories that have said good and bad about that. How about you? Good? Bad? Both?"

"All good, actually. I loved it here. I loved living on the farm, I loved that everyone knew everyone else—it was all just one great big family to me," Jenna said, taking a sip of her wine.

"Then why did you leave?" he asked, doing the same.

"I'd always planned to leave for a while, for college—

the local college didn't offer what I needed. But I'd also always planned to come back as soon as I could. This was such a great place to grow up, it was where I wanted to have and raise my own kids."

"But you were away for how long?"

"Too long—ten years," she said, unable to keep the disdain for that fact out of her voice.

"Was there something keeping you away that was out of your control?"

Jenna knew her tone had opened the door to that question. But there was a limit to what she was willing to tell this man, so she said, "Things just happen. We make choices—not always good ones—and sometimes the tide carries you farther and farther out to sea. It makes it tough to get back to shore."

"Shore being Northbridge?"

"And my family...."

"Were you at odds with them?"

"No," she said firmly. Because the truth was bad enough. She didn't want him to think something worse had kept her away. "It was just... Because I let other things take precedence, it was hard to get home. So I didn't make it back as often as I wanted to—barely once a year and sometimes even longer than that would go by before I could get back. If that hadn't been the case..."

She took another sip of wine, because she needed some bolstering to talk about this.

"What?" Ian urged.

Jenna shrugged. "If I'd been able to visit more often, if I'd been able to move back two or three years ago the way I'd planned, I might have seen the indications of my mother's heart problems and had them addressed before she ended up having the attack that killed her."

"She didn't tell you she was feeling bad?"

"My parents didn't believe in burdening their kids with their problems—that's what my father said when I asked why neither he nor Mom had said anything. So no, no one told me Mom had been getting short of breath, tiring easily, that her coloring wasn't great. No one told me that Dad was having more and more trouble taking care of the farm, so it wasn't making the kind of profit it needed to. I didn't know they were slipping behind on the taxes. If I'd been here, if I'd known, maybe I could have done something…."

Jenna wasn't sure how this conversation had gotten so heavy, but she was battling her own emotions and Ian was watching her intently, a frown pulling his eyebrows together, his expression very somber.

"That's a whole lot of guilt you're carrying around," he said softly. "Is that what's behind the sticking point to keep the farm a farm? Are you trying to make up for what you didn't do along the way, by keeping it some kind of monument to your parents?"

Jenna shook her head. "No, that isn't it at all. My dad loved the farm and being a farmer. He was proud of what he did, of the contribution it made. He believed that the farmer was the backbone of this country, and he liked being a part of that. He wanted it to continue, even if it wasn't his own family doing it, so his last wish—his last request of me—was that his farm remain a farm. Simple as that. And that's what I'm trying to help happen. If I don't sell to you for your training facility, and you don't buy it at auction, there's at least the chance that someone else might buy it and maintain it as a working farm, the way my Dad wanted, and that's really all I'm trying to accomplish."

"Now *I* feel guilty!"

"Good!" Jenna said with a laugh that helped make her feel better. "Does that mean you'll back off?"

He flinched. "It was me who brought your place to the attention of the powers-that-be—for that I'm completely to blame. But in my defense, I had no idea there were these kinds of personal and emotional issues on the other side of it."

"And now that you do, you'll back off?" Jenna repeated hopefully.

"Even now that I do, it's too late. The moneymen, the land people, the contractors—everyone connected with the project—has agreed that your property is ideal on all counts. That takes it out of my hands. I'm sorry."

He might have been a very convincing liar, but Jenna had the sense that he genuinely meant that apology.

"And even if I went to my father at this point and said let's let it be," he continued after a pause, "I'd get shot down. The first thing my old man would say is that there's no guarantee that if the property goes to auction, it'll stay a farm. Potentially the Monarchs would just lose the best site for their training center to some housing developer or something."

Jenna knew that was a possibility, too. But still, she was trying to hang on to what hope she could. For her father's sake.

"I guess it just isn't possible for us to come down on the same side of this," she concluded. "And I think you might be trying to find my weak spot or something—"

"I'm not," he protested.

But before either of them could say more on the subject, Chase appeared at the entrance of the showcase. "There you are, Ian," he said. "I've been looking for you."

Chase paused to say hello to Jenna, to tell her how nice she looked and tease her that it was nothing like a new mom was supposed to look.

After they'd joked back and forth for a few minutes, Chase's gaze went to Ian again. "I wanted to introduce you around—there are a lot of people who want to meet you."

"That sounds like a good idea," Jenna said pushing away from the desk and seizing the opening to put an end to being alone with Ian. "I need to check on Abby and make sure she isn't giving the sitters a hard time, so I'll leave you two to that."

And with those words, she took her wine and left Ian to his brother.

Jenna had hoped that she'd gotten her fill of Ian Kincaid during their brief first encounter at the grand opening. And certainly after checking on Abby and then rejoining the party, she tried to enjoy it without giving him another thought.

But trying was one thing.

Succeeding was something else…

Again she'd liked talking to him—even talking about something that they were at odds over. And not giving him another thought was impossible. The best she accomplished as the evening wore on was to stay away from him, and since he didn't approach her, that wasn't difficult to do.

But he *was* still there, for her to catch sight of repeatedly, for her to hear addressing a group behind her, for her to even get a chance to stare at when he made a toast to Chase, Logan and Hadley to congratulate them on the opening of the Northbridge branch of Mackey and McKendrick Furniture Designs and wish them continued success.

Finally conceding that she couldn't seem to stop being ultra-aware of the man at every turn, Jenna decided it was time to go home to get away from the phenomenon.

So, she found Meg, assured her that the party had been terrific and said good-night.

Inside the main house, the older kids were still playing but the babies—Abby included—were sound asleep.

The slumbering infant wasn't disturbed in the slightest by Jenna putting on her coat and then buckling her into the baby carrier that also acted as a car seat.

It was when Jenna headed for the front door to leave that Ian suddenly showed up, seemingly from out of nowhere, to open that door for her.

"Let me help you," was all he said while they were within the babysitters' earshot, taking the carrier from her as they headed outside.

But once Jenna had strapped Abby's car seat in and closed the rear door of her SUV, she turned to find Ian with one arm lying across the rooftop and looking intently at her.

"I couldn't let you leave without making a confession…"

"I understand it's good for the soul—what do you need to confess?"

"The reason I had the Realtor bring me out to your house on Saturday was because I knew you were going to be there, and I wanted to finally meet you. I wanted to get the ball rolling to try to figure out what was keeping you from selling the farm to us, to see if I could find an opening and something I could use to convince you that you should."

"It was all about business," Jenna summed up, fighting how demoralizing it was to hear that.

"I'll admit that that's been in the back of my mind at the start of every time we've met up, but somehow…" He shook his head, he shrugged. "Somehow I completely lose sight of that about two minutes in, because I just like talking to you."

He said that sincerely, but it was the fact that it seemed to confuse him that was more of a selling point.

"Okay," she allowed, feeling a bit less deflated.

"And tonight, it was really nice of you to keep me company when I needed it. I honestly wasn't angling for anything. I don't want you to go away believing that you did a good deed, and I took advantage of you for it, because we did end up talking about the farm. If anything, finding out what's behind you *not* selling to us just shot the hell out of my wanting your place."

Jenna nodded her head in response.

"I also want you to know that I understand that—when it comes to the farm—you're just trying to do what your father wanted. It's a position I'm in a lot between work and the family, so I can appreciate it." He gave her a lopsided smile, "But when it comes to your farm, at this point, I really am stuck. Sympathetic, but stuck. And yet here we are, in this small town—"

"And we're going to run into each other," Jenna supplied, assuming where he was going with this.

"We are. And I don't want to be enemies with someone I like talking to. I don't want us to have to dodge each other. I don't want you to hate that I'm at the same restaurant or at any of the preliminary things going on for Shannon and Dag's wedding or the wedding itself on Sunday."

So there were going to be a lot of places they encountered each other. She hadn't been thinking beyond tonight.

"I'd really like to feel free to sit and have a glass of wine and talk to you the way we did earlier," he said. "I *don't* want us to be uncomfortable around each other. So, what if we just set this aside—is there any chance of that? Can we agree that we both know where the other is coming from, what we have to do and why, but sort of remove ourselves from it? Do you think that's possible?"

"As in—you've made your offer on the farm, I've refused it—end of subject. You will likely be bidding on it at the auction, and if I don't have another buyer by then, you'll probably get it for your training center, and there's nothing I can do about it—end of subject. So, can we just let the cards fall where they may and separate ourselves from it?"

"I know it's a lot and that, in your position, I'm asking you to be the much bigger person about it, but yeah, could you do that?"

Beyond standing her ground and refusing to sell to

anyone who would not agree to maintain the farm, there genuinely wasn't much she could do about the ultimate outcome, and she had already had to accept that. And while she didn't like that Ian was playing a role in it, as she gazed up into that face the porch light was glazing in gold, that face that looked so eager for her to grant him this request, she just didn't have the inclination to deny it.

Besides, she'd learned tonight that worrying about where he was every minute, in order to make sure she stayed away from him, only added to her heightened awareness of him and compounded the problem.

And okay, yes, although she shouldn't, she liked the idea of sitting and talking with him, having another glass of wine with him. If the occasion arose…

"I get to be the 'bigger person'?" she said, as if that were the clincher.

He smiled a hundred-watt smile. "And I'll say it to anyone who asks."

"Okay, then. The farm issue goes in one box, you and I coexisting here goes in another box."

His smile went to a thousand watts. "You're just my brother's partner's wife's best friend, and I'm just—"

"My best friend's husband's partner's brother," Jenna played along with the ridiculousness of those lengthy labels.

"And we can have wine and talk and maybe even dance at the wedding?"

"If not before—there *is* the Spring Fling Dance on Friday night," Jenna joked.

"Oh, yeah, I think I heard something about that…."

Ian said, as if she'd just sparked his interest in the event. "But no matter what, we're okay—you and I?"

It seemed to mean so much to him that it made Jenna grin, too. "We're okay. You and I," she confirmed.

"Good," he said, as if it were a relief.

Then he slid that arm off the rooftop and took hold of her shoulder to slightly squeeze it.

Once again that simple touch caused more things to erupt in her than it should have, and as she gazed up into that handsome face, what skipped through her mind were thoughts of him kissing her.

Which, of course, she would never let happen.

It was one thing to agree that they could be civil—friendly, even. But there was nothing in there about kissing!

And yet…

There was a quiet little part of her that couldn't stop thinking about it….

So she moved to open the driver's side door. And Ian took his hand away—leaving her sorrier to lose his touch than was appropriate or called for.

"I should go before Abby gets cold," she said then.

"Right," Ian Kincaid agreed, completely opening her door and holding it for her while she got behind the wheel, put the keys in the ignition and started the engine.

They said good-night as he closed the door and stepped to a clear spot so she could maneuver her SUV from the line of other cars parked in the drive.

And the entire way back to her house, Jenna made sure to remind herself that Ian had admitted to exactly what she'd suspected of him—that what took precedence with him was pleasing his father. And not merely the way she was trying to grant her own father's dying wish but in his everyday dealings.

The big red warning flare…

And she needed to heed it.

Which she had every intention of doing.

Even if she was having trouble forgetting what he'd looked like standing beside her SUV at the moment that kissing had crossed her mind.

And maybe wishing just a little that he might actually have given it a try….

Chapter Four

It was not every day that Jenna looked up from her kitchen sink to peer through the window and discover a sports celebrity in her backyard.

But as Tuesday afternoon turned into Tuesday evening, that's what happened.

She'd finished her shift at the hospital, picked up Abby from Meg's, come home and changed into her most comfortable jeans and a comfy, white, crew-necked T-shirt. Then she'd brushed out her hair and caught it in a ponytail at her crown and decided to fix a pan of lasagna for dinner.

With the lasagna in the oven and Abby playing with pots and pans that the infant had dragged out of a cupboard, Jenna was doing the dishes she'd used to put the lasagna together. And lo and behold, football great, Morgan Kincaid, appeared from around the corner of her house.

With Ian not far behind him.

Finished with rinsing her dishes, Jenna turned off the water. Morgan Kincaid was looking steadfastly in the opposite direction, but Ian caught sight of Jenna through the kitchen window and came up to it.

Since the weather was still setting record-high temperatures for March, and the heat from the oven had added additional warmth to the kitchen, the window was open for him to say through the screen, "Hi. I rang the doorbell, but there was no answer."

"I must have been running the garbage disposal—I didn't hear it," Jenna said, in lieu of a greeting.

"And the voicemail I left—did you get that?"

"I haven't taken my phone out of my purse since I got home. That would make it somewhere near the front door. I've been upstairs and in here—I didn't know I *had* a voicemail."

"My father was flying home and decided to make a quick—and unannounced—stop here. He's only seen the place in pictures and decided on the spur of the moment that he should take a look at the real thing. I couldn't get hold of the Realtor, so I called to get your permission to bring him over, but when there was no answer I just left the message. I hope you don't mind, but I brought him, anyway. If it's a problem, we'll leave...."

Jenna had two thoughts about what Ian had just said—first of all, despite the fact that she hadn't agreed to a showing of the farm right now, Ian's father was getting his way. Secondly, she had the impression that if she said their visit was a problem for her, Ian would make sure it ended.

It was tempting to test that impression and see for

herself if Ian could wield that kind of power over his father, but it seemed slightly petty, too.

And because she was also in the throes of a little, secret excitement at seeing Ian, she said, "It's no big deal. You can show him around."

"He doesn't want to see inside the house, if that helps. He just wants the lay of the land."

Ian hadn't noticed that his father had just joined him at the window.

"Hello," Morgan Kincaid said over his son's shoulder.

Glancing back at him, Ian said, "Dad, this is Jenna Bowen, the owner of the place. Jenna, this is my father, Morgan Kincaid."

It wasn't as if Jenna wouldn't have recognized the still athletically built older man whose face had been in the news, on magazine covers and in local and national newspapers for decades. Morgan Kincaid had made nothing if not a splash. He'd first come into the limelight in college football. Then in professional football as one of the NFL's best—ever players with numerous Most Valuable Player Awards, quarterbacking teams to three Super Bowl victories and ending up in the Pro Football Hall Of Fame.

When he'd retired from the game, he'd turned his sports fame and fortune into the Kincaid Corporation which was a conglomerate of retail centers, rental and hotel properties, car dealerships, restaurants and, now, the Montana Monarchs NFL expansion team.

"Nice to meet you, Mr. Kincaid," Jenna said simply.

"Please, call me Morgan," the silver-haired man responded. "My son has told me about your situation here and why your farm is up for sale—his conscience is eating at him for having done such a good job convincing us that your place is the right spot for the training center. But he *has* convinced us, so I hope you'll consider our offer to buy before the auction."

"Sorry," Jenna said with a stubborn shake of her head.

Morgan Kincaid nodded, but she could tell by his implacable expression that her refusal changed nothing for him. He would buy her out or he would take the farm at the auction, but either way he would have what he wanted—that was what his attitude projected.

However, he did say, "Would you like us to leave?"

Jenna tossed a glance to Ian and said, "We've come to an understanding about things, so no. Do what you need to do."

"I appreciate that," Morgan Kincaid said. Then he added a perfunctory, "Nice to meet you," and turned his back to her to resume looking out at the rest of the property.

"Thanks," Ian said to Jenna. Then, with a smile that was just for her, he leaned nearer to the screen to add, "I don't know what you're cooking in there but put me on the reservation list, will you?"

"Sure," she said, believing he was joking and so joking in return.

He winked at her. A charming, wicked wink that made her smile, too, and seemed to enlist her in some sort of conspiracy—although she had no idea what they were conspiring to do.

Then he turned around and began to describe for his father the best positioning for the fields, the administration building, the conditioning center and the rest of the facility he had planned.

Jenna considered closing the window so she couldn't hear what was being said as she returned to her cleanup. But it was still her house, and the kitchen was still overly warm, which was the reason she'd opened the window in the first place. So, she opted not to.

While she didn't particularly want to know about the training center, as she loaded the dishwasher, she found herself inordinately interested in what passed between the two men and in the dynamics of their relationship.

Ian outlined what was clearly a project he knew inside and out and answered every question his father asked, but there was no obsequiousness in the way he reacted to Morgan Kincaid. There was no fawning, no groveling, no kowtowing. There was nothing in Ian's actions that reminded her of her ex-husband with his mother—which was what she'd expected to see. There wasn't even the kind of deference to a boss that someone else who worked for the mighty Morgan Kincaid might have shown.

Instead, Ian spoke to his father as if they were equals, and it occurred to Jenna that maybe that was an advantage of being the boss's son.

But he admitted himself that he goes to extremes to please his father, and they are here even though he didn't get my permission first, because that's what his father wanted, she reminded herself.

"I can take you over to look at the other property, too," she heard Ian say then. "I know the cost is higher, and there's more leveling that would need to be done, but I have some ideas—"

"No, I think your instincts were right from the start—

this is the place," Morgan Kincaid decreed, obviously having the final say.

Jenna appreciated that Ian had given it a try, though. Then the elder Kincaid switched gears, and Jenna's interest was piqued all over again. "Have you talked to Chelsea?"

Chelsea?

"Two nights ago," Ian said.

"Did you call her or did she call you?"

"She called me."

"Good, good. Any chance she'll come back early?"

"She's on a photo shoot in Paris, Dad, so no. That's her job, and she won't come back until she's finished."

"You could take a long weekend and—"

"I don't have the time for that."

"Your job is to look after the best interests of the Monarchs, and the Monarchs need sponsorship. Revenue. A football franchise and a brewery? That's a perfect match," Morgan Kincaid said. "You and Chelsea together, with Chelsea working for her father and sticking around more to be with you, would seal the deal between the Monarchs and Tanner Brewery—I'll throw you the biggest wedding Montana has ever seen."

Chelsea? Photo shoot in Paris? Wedding?

"Drop it, Dad," Ian said then. "Chelsea and I are friendly—that's all. I'm doing what you and her father want as far as trying to convince her that it might be good for her to be the spokeswoman for Tanner Brewery if it comes on board with the Monarchs. We have some musical tastes in common, but that's it—no romance. She's not interested in me, I'm not interested in her."

"But romance could develop—how bad would it be?

She's a model, she's beautiful. If *she* called *you* from Paris that means she likes you," the former football star pointed out hopefully.

Ian laughed wryly. "We have the same taste in music. We're exchanging playlists. That's it. We're *friends* exchanging playlists," he repeated slowly, seemingly for emphasis.

"But a long weekend in Paris—on the company's dime—things could become more than that…"

"Or I could just get Tanner Brewery to sign on for sponsorship because it's good business."

"But the two of you together—that would lock in permanent sponsorship—"

"Uh-huh," Ian said as if it just wasn't worth arguing about.

But still Jenna couldn't shake the fact that his father wanted him hooked up with whomever this Chelsea was.

And there *was* a Chelsea.

There was a Chelsea…

Jenna had no idea why that disturbed her so much but she suddenly wanted the Kincaids to leave.

Go away! Get off my property while it's still my property! she thought, wishing she could play frontier woman, pull out a shotgun and run them off.

But just then Morgan Kincaid looked at his watch and said, "I have to get going—there's a charity thing tonight in Billings and I'm the guest speaker."

The older man headed around the house and as Ian followed him he glanced at the window again. When he spotted Jenna this time he raised a palm as if to wave goodbye. But that open palm quickly closed around a single index finger pointed as if he was signaling for something.

Jenna had no idea what that meant, but responded with a halfhearted wave of her own just as he disappeared around the side of the house.

A sudden chill made her decide to close the window above the sink before she wiped down her countertops. And while she did she couldn't get the echo of another woman's name out of her head.

Chelsea. Chelsea. Chelsea…

Was Ian Kincaid seeing someone?

He had said he was just being friendly. That he wasn't interested in the woman and the feeling was mutual. That he was just exchanging playlists with her to build rapport. So it didn't seem like it. But that *was* what his father wanted….

Why should I care one way or another? Jenna chastised herself.

She shouldn't. She didn't. There wasn't a single reason why it should matter in the slightest if Ian Kincaid was engaged and on the verge of marrying ten women!

The doorbell rang just then and jolted her slightly because she'd been so lost in thinking about Ian and his involvement with this Chelsea person.

Belatedly, it occurred to her that that single finger he'd raised might have meant one minute. One minute before he returned. And that could be him at her front door.

Abandoning her sponge and knowing the mischief Abby could get into being left alone for even a moment, Jenna scooped the baby up into her arms and went to the front door.

Sure enough, Ian was standing on the front porch.

She could see his car parked in the drive that led to the house, but there was no sign of his father.

"Reservation for one," he said, as if he were at a restaurant.

Was that what the single finger had meant?

But *Chelsea* was still on Jenna's mind and it made her tone a bit aloof. "I thought you were kidding," she said.

"I was. I am," he assured, frowning slightly, as if she'd confused him. Then he seemed to relax a little and said, "My father is gone, I just wanted to hang back and tell you thanks for letting me show him the place and to apologize again for the drop-in."

"No problem," Jenna answered.

"Un," Abby said then, holding out her arms to him through the screen.

"Hi, Abby," he said affectionately, giving the baby a big smile and holding the tip of one finger to the screen for her.

That went a long way in melting Jenna's coolness, and a little voice in the back of her mind said, *They are just exchanging playlists...*

And he did look fantastic—he was wearing the first pair of jeans she'd seen him in, and what the man did to a few yards of denim was sinful. He also had on a sky-blue shirt that brought out the blue of his eyes, and a bluish-gray sport coat that finished the look of city-meets-country style with more sexy flair than he had any right to.

It all worked to take the starch out of her, and before she had even made the decision consciously, she heard herself say, "I do have enough lasagna for half a dozen people if you want to stay…."

"Don't say it unless you mean it, because I'll take you up on it," he warned.

But she did mean it. Even though she wished she didn't and wasn't quite sure why she did.

There's someone else, she reminded herself as she pushed open the screen door. *He's duty- and otherwise-bound to do his father's bidding, plus there's someone named Chelsea in his life. Someone he seems to like just fine and his father wants him to marry....*

But what she said was, "Come in."

Ian didn't require any more persuasion than that to step across the threshold and close the door behind himself.

Again Abby said, "Un," and leaned toward him with outstretched arms.

"Let him take his coat off first," Jenna told the baby.

Ian shrugged out of it and hung it on one of the four pegs that lined the chair rail on the wall behind the door.

Then he took Abby, who once more curled her arm around his neck with an air of possessiveness, just as a timer sounded from the kitchen.

"That's for the lasagna," Jenna informed him, retracing her steps down the hallway beside the staircase to the kitchen with Ian and Abby following behind.

"Sit down," she said as she opened the oven door, removed the foil that covered the lasagna and then set the timer for another fifteen minutes. "I have salad and bread to go with this. I need to set the table and get Abby's dinner going—she won't touch lasagna—"

"You made it just for yourself?"

"I was craving it."

"Is there anything I can do to help?"

"No, just sit."

"I should let Hadley know I won't be there for dinner," he said, as if that had just occurred to him. Then he pulled out one of the spindle-backed chairs and sat with Abby on his lap at the round pedestal table. He took his cell phone from his shirt pocket and made the call while Jenna poured Abby a sippy-cup of milk and set it on the table in front of her.

Jenna was taking two adult-size glasses out of the cupboard when Ian got off the phone. "Will they miss you?" she asked.

"Nah," he assured. "They'll probably like having some time alone."

Jenna nodded, held up the two water glasses and said, "Water, iced tea, lemonade or soda?"

"What, no Chianti? What kind of Italian restaurant is this?" he joked again.

"Lasagna for one I could justify, but a bottle of wine for one? That seemed like a waste." Although now she was sorry she didn't have it to offer.

"Water is fine," Ian said, helping Abby with her sippy-cup when she couldn't quite reach it.

As she began to make the salad, Jenna said, "Sooo, your father didn't see any demerits in putting the training center here?"

"Sorry," Ian said, sounding genuinely contrite.

"And now that he's given his stamp of approval, that's it, huh? Because he calls the shots…."

"We weren't going to talk about this anymore, remember?" he said. "It's out of our hands. What will be, will be, and we're separating ourselves from it when we're together."

As if their being together was something special?

That was a dangerous thought, which Jenna shooed away.

But she *had* agreed that they wouldn't talk about the farm, so she conceded to his reminder by asking him how his day had gone and telling him about her own as she dressed the salad, sliced bread, made Abby's dinner, took the lasagna out and cut it into squares.

Then, with everything ready to eat, Ian put Abby in the high chair, and Jenna tied the infant's bib around her neck. By the time she and Ian sat down to eat, it struck Jenna that this was all very family-like. And that it was nice.

For this one night. This one night that had happened on the spur of the moment. And wouldn't ever happen again.

Those were things she felt she should keep in mind, before she liked this whole scenario too much.

Abby had a sauceless version of the lasagna, which was basically macaroni and cheeses. And since the baby was intent on participating in her meals, there were two spoons—one for Abby to use awkwardly and messily and the other for Jenna to use to actually get some of the food in Abby's mouth.

She did that first—persuading Abby to taste her mac and cheese—before she served Ian and herself the rest of the meal and got into her usual rhythm of alternating a bite for herself and a bite for Abby.

After Ian had tasted the lasagna and deemed it even

better than it smelled, and Jenna had thanked him, she searched for a way to get the attention off herself.

"Tell me about your dad," she said, going in that direction to accomplish her goal.

Ian laughed. "Where would you like me to start?"

"At the beginning—but not with the stuff that everybody knows. How did he get to be your father in the first place—I mean, how did you get from Northbridge to being the son of one of the biggest sports stars in the whole country?"

"Adoption," Ian said with a smile.

Jenna rolled her eyes at him. "But how did that adoption come about? I know that you and your twin—"

"Hutch."

"—were orphaned along with Chase, Shannon and a half sister when your parents were killed in a car accident. I know that Meg's grandfather—Reverend Perry—was instrumental in finding homes for all but Chase. But I heard something about Morgan Kincaid not being your first adoptive dad...."

"Right. My mother was married to a man named Tony Bruno at the time—he was my first adoptive father. They were willing to take both Hutch and I so we wouldn't be separated—that went a long way in persuading the powers-that-be to give us to them. We were two months old at the time."

"So what happened to Tony Bruno?"

"He and my mother moved to Billings right after they adopted us. But the way my mother tells it, Tony Bruno didn't turn out to be much of a breadwinner or a father or a husband, and they were divorced before Hutch and I were as old as Abby is."

"Bi?" Abby said, apparently hearing her name and deciding to offer Ian a bite of her dinner.

"Mmm, thank you," Ian said, pretending to take the bite the infant offered and not showing any revulsion at the gooey mess the fifteen-month-old wanted to share.

Then he went back to his story. "My mother met Morgan Kincaid within a month after her divorce was final—through mutual friends. They hit it off, got married six months after that, and he wanted to raise us as his own kids, not as stepkids. Giving up parental rights got Tony Bruno off the hook for child support—which my mother says he wasn't paying anyway—so he agreed to that and willingly stepped out of the picture. Hutch and I were two years and three months old by that time—not old enough to remember him, and since he never came around after that, Morgan Kincaid became my adoptive father and the only father I actually know."

"And what's he like as a father?" Jenna asked. Having eaten her fill, she settled back to focus on Abby and her conversation with Ian.

"Morgan Kincaid as a father..." Ian shrugged. "There's always been good and bad. Hutch and I, in particular, got a lot of his attention and some of that was fun. On the other hand, it put more pressure on us than either of us liked. And we were also in the public eye—trotted out for everything—"

"Everything like...football games?"

"Oh yeah, definitely for football games—we had to be front and center for every one of those. But we were on display for everything else, too. Being a family man was a big deal to my father. He doesn't approve of the playboy-sports-figure persona, he believes that everything to do with football should be wholesome, that there's a responsibility to be a good role model when you're a prominent sports figure. Being a father, being connected with charities, fundraising, politics—those were what he wanted to be known for. Which was part of why Hutch and I and Lacey—our younger sister who was also adopted—were paraded out as the poster children to advocate for adoption."

"It sounds as if you didn't appreciate that...."

"I hated it," he said bluntly, and she could tell by the sobering of his expression that he really had.

"Did you not want it known that you were adopted?" she guessed.

"It was always out in the open, but making such a big deal of it just...I don't know...made it tough to forget about. It made it tough for me to shake the feeling that we were somehow acquisitions or disposable or something."

"Oh, that's not good...." Jenna said in a sort of verbal flinch, feeling sorry for the young Ian and hating the thought that Abby could ever think such a thing.

"Don't get me wrong—my mother and father didn't do anything to cause that in me. They always said we were more special because they chose us, that they'd had to prove how much they wanted us to get us—that kind of thing. But—"

"I could see where your father making you the poster kid for adoption might have made you feel like an acquisition. But do you think Tony Bruno giving you up so easily contributed to you feeling disposable?"

Ian seemed to consider that as he finished his dinner

and then sat back to watch her try to persuade Abby to take a few more bites.

"I don't know," he finally said. "That's an interesting point that never occurred to me. I mean, I was too young to have any memory of the guy at all, so it wasn't as if I felt any kind of loss that the first man to adopt me bailed. But now that you mention it, I wonder if somewhere in my kid brain the fact that he seemed to have no problem passing us on to the next guy gave me that sense. I just know that I had it. That after my mom died—"

"What did she die of?"

"She had a brain aneurysm—apparently it was like a ticking time bomb in her head, which no one ever knew she had. But I was eleven when she died and I know I worried myself sick that if Mom was gone, Dad might not want us around anymore, either."

"That just breaks my heart," Jenna told him.

"All I know is that I always felt as if I had to not only be grateful for what I was given, but prove how grateful I was. And to earn being my father's son."

"By doing what your dad wanted of you?" Another guess.

Ian nodded. "In a lot of respects, yeah."

"I can't imagine feeling like that. I never felt like I had to earn my place as my parent's child. Or even go to any great lengths to please either of them. Doing what I'm doing at the farm is really the only extra step I ever felt I needed to take to please my dad or my mom."

"Maybe because your parents were your birth parents. That's why I only want kids who are my own. I never want kids who aren't, and who might have the thoughts and feelings I had."

"What about your brother? Did he—*does* he—feel the same way?"

"Hutch? No. We may be twins, but we're pretty different. At least, we always were. I haven't seen him in almost six years now, so I probably shouldn't speak to what he does or doesn't feel, but I know he didn't feel that way before."

"You haven't seen your twin brother in six years?" Jenna marveled as she gave up trying to get Abby to eat any more, and wiped the baby's face with her bib before taking it off. "I thought twins were always close…."

"Yeah, that was one of the casualties of having Morgan Kincaid as a father."

"How so?" Jenna asked, hoping she wasn't prying too much.

"There was a huge push for both Hutch and I to follow in our father's footsteps. We were enrolled in Little League football the minute we were old enough to be and even before that he had us in the yard every minute he could spare, teaching us to throw the ball, play the game, to compete—always to compete. 'Competition is what makes men strong'—that was my father's motto."

"Your father pitted the two of you against each other?"

"In every way he could dream up."

"So did you end up more rivals than brothers?"

"I'd say about half and half, but there was definitely rivalry. Too much for us to be as close as other twins I've known. But Dad figured the rivalry improved us both since he was also determined that we be individuals… Being twins did not give us an unusually strong bond, no."

"And now you haven't seen your brother in six years...."

"I guess it stands to reason that eventually there would be a straw that broke the camel's back, and there was," Ian said.

But that was all he said, leaving her hanging.

Or maybe he would have said more, except that Abby chose that moment to become fussy and fidgety.

"Don't get tired out yet," Jenna cajoled, taking the baby out of the high chair to place on her lap. "You still need your bath tonight before you can go to bed."

"I probably drew this meal out longer than it would have taken otherwise, haven't I? And I know you worked today, and then you made this great food and now you still have to get Abby to bed. How about if I clean up down here as restitution for inviting myself to dinner while you give Abby a bath?"

"Oh, I couldn't let you do that."

"Sure you could. It's the least I can do. Just tell me what to do with your leftovers and leave it all to me."

It still took Jenna a few back-and-forths before she conceded to having a guest clean her kitchen, but Ian wouldn't take no for an answer.

Then, too, she thought as she gave Abby a quick bath and got the baby to bed, the idea of going back downstairs and having a little time alone with Ian wasn't altogether awful.

But after she got the fifteen-month-old settled and drifting off to sleep and descended the stairs, she found Ian with his coat already on, leaning one shoulder against the front door waiting for her.

"You're leaving?" she said, trying not to sound unhappy.

"Not without saying thanks or goodbye, but yeah, I figured you probably wanted some peace and quiet."

And maybe he wanted to call *Chelsea*...

But as if he knew what Jenna was thinking, he added, "And I have to go over the talk I'm giving at your town meeting tomorrow night. Will you be there?"

Was there a hopeful note in his voice? Jenna wondered as she reached the bottom of the steps and met him at the door to stand facing him.

"I planned to be," she said, not revealing that the reason she'd planned to be there was to learn how much more money had been raised for the save-the-farm fund.

"Would you let me buy you dinner afterwards?" he asked.

That surprised her, and he must have seen it on her face because he smiled.

"Or does it look bad if you're seen fraternizing with the enemy?" he joked. "If it does, I could meet you back here with take-out…."

She wasn't worried about being seen fraternizing with the enemy, but the thought of ending up alone here with him did have some appeal. Especially since he was cutting tonight shorter than she wished he was.

Not that it should matter….

"I did promise my babysitter that I'd be home right after the meeting—she has a chemistry test the next day."

"But you'll let me in if I show up bearing pizza or burgers or Chinese food?"

What about Chelsea? she was tempted to say.

But that would have revealed the fact that she'd eavesdropped on him and his father, and she didn't want to do that. And once more she thought, *Just friends exchanging playlists...*

"I might not turn away the bearer of such offerings," she allowed.

He smiled but committed to no more than he already had. Instead he just studied her, continuing to smile as if he liked what he saw.

Then he said, "Thanks for letting me barge in on your dinner tonight. It really was the best lasagna I've ever eaten."

"I'm glad you liked it."

"And the company, too…." he said quietly.

Somehow it seemed as if she would be exposing too much to tell him she'd also enjoyed his company. To such an extent that she was hating that he was leaving. In order to hide that, though, she hid behind levity and said, "Abby is known far and wide for her stimulating conversations."

"And generously sharing her food," he played along. "Oh, and you're not so bad yourself," he added to tease her.

"I just follow Abby's lead."

His smile stretched into a grin as he continued to study her, his gaze settling on her eyes after a moment.

He reached out and took her upper arm, rubbing up and down, gently, sending a glittery sensation all the way to her fingertips.

Then his hand stopped to close around her arm in a tender but firm grip that could easily have gone to pulling her in closer….

And suddenly there was something different in the air around them. Something that caused Jenna to think about kissing. But not in the way she'd thought about kissing the night before. This wasn't as whimsical, this seemed to have more foundation.

The air around them was charged, and kissing seemed like more than a fleeting thought in her mind alone. It actually seemed possible.

Maybe even about to happen…

Especially since he was leaning just a bit more toward her…

Her chin rose a fraction of an inch—but only in a questioning sort of gesture, she told herself. Not to accommodate a kiss. Not to encourage one. Not to meet him partway. It was purely coincidence that that tilted chin accomplished those things, too.

But then it struck her that last night, when she'd thought about him trying to kiss her, she'd thought that she wouldn't let him.

And tonight she wasn't so sure that was still true…

If he tried, she just might…

He was still looking into her eyes, searching them, holding them. He was coming ever so slightly nearer…

Oh, yeah, if he tried to kiss her she was going to let him…

But then he gave her arm the same kind of squeeze he'd given her shoulder the previous evening, straightened up and let go, so he could reach for the doorknob and open the door instead.

"I really better get going," he said in a quiet voice that was deeper than it had been before. "I'll see you tomorrow night—at the meeting and then here later."

Just to pay her back for the meal she'd fed him, Jenna told herself. There was nothing more to it than him being friendly. He had a *Chelsea....*

"Thanks again for tonight," he added.

"Sure," Jenna said.

Still, his eyes were on her and she had the impression that he was having second thoughts about just walking away.

But in the end, that's what he did, muttering a simple, "Good night."

"Good night," Jenna called after him, watching him go out to his car, drinking in that parting view of broad shoulders and long, muscular legs.

And again she chanted to herself: *Chelsea, Chelsea, Chelsea, there is a Chelsea...*

A Chelsea his father wanted him to be with. In the future, even if they weren't together now...

But tonight he maneuvered himself into being with me, she couldn't help thinking.

Tonight, he'd made plans to be with her tomorrow night, too.

And tonight, unless she was mistaken, he'd come very close to kissing her.

A kiss she would have let him have.

A kiss she would have returned.

Even knowing that she shouldn't.

Because what she discovered, in the immense disappointment that came over her as she watched him drive away, was that she really, really, really had wanted him to forget everything—the farm, his father, whoever Chelsea was.

And just kiss her like crazy....

Chapter Five

"Molly-The-Dolly—she's one of my favorites," Jenna informed Abby after the fifteen-month-old had chosen the toy from her downstairs toy box on Wednesday evening.

Jenna had fed Abby dinner, given her a bath and gotten her ready for bed, along with undertaking some of her own concentrated primping for the Town Meeting tonight. She'd made sure to start early enough so that she would have some time to spend with Abby before the babysitter arrived. Becky would be putting Abby to bed, and Jenna wouldn't get to see her again until morning. Every minute she didn't spend with Abby, she missed her.

So now, with everything finished, Jenna had taken Abby downstairs and encouraged her to get a toy for them to play with. Abby had chosen the rag doll that taught how to button buttons, zip zippers, tie ties, snap snaps, buckle buckles and stick Velcro. Jenna also used it to teach basics, so when she took Abby to sit with her on the couch and settled Abby on her lap, she said, "Where's Molly's hair?"

Abby yanked the doll up by its yarn-loop locks, and Jenna laughed. "That's right, that's Molly's hair. Where's Abby's hair?"

The baby was more gentle in patting the top of her own head.

"That's right—you're so smart! Where's my hair?"

Abby pointed to Jenna's hair—freshly washed and scrunched into a full mass of curls she'd caught at her nape. It seemed slightly dressier than usual, without being overly obvious that she'd put some thought, time and effort into it. The same thought, time and effort she'd taken with all aspects of her appearance tonight because she knew she'd be seeing Ian. At the meeting and then later, too. Back here…

"Where are Molly's eyes?" she asked Abby.

Abby poked one of the doll's felt eyes.

"Very good. Where are your eyes?"

Abby showed her.

"And my eyes?" Complete with mascara and a dusting of barely visible shadow.

Abby pointed to Jenna's eyes.

They did noses, and then went on to Molly's mouth which was comprised of much brighter, red felt lips than Jenna's pale lip gloss had provided her.

Jenna's tan slacks and the teal blue blouse she wore over a cream-colored tank top were less gaudy than the doll's multi-colored outfit, too.

"Where are Molly's hands?" she asked next.

Abby jumped ahead and showed her own hand—palm out, fingers splayed.

Jenna laughed again. "That's Abby's hand. And how many fingers does she have?" Jenna counted them, gently pinching the tip of each one as she did.

"How about toes? Does Abby have toes like Molly?"

The infant's toes were concealed in the feet of her one-piece pajamas but still Abby grabbed them, rocking back against Jenna in the process.

Once more Jenna laughed, praised the baby and then did This-Little-Piggy through the pajama feet.

But it was nearing Abby's bedtime, and she was clearly weary because she stayed cuddled against Jenna, tucking Molly under one arm and fiddling with the untied ribbon in the doll's hair rather than giving Jenna more access to the toy.

Jenna got the message and was content to merely sit and hold Abby, to snuggle with her, to talk to her.

"Becky will be here in a few minutes," she told the child. "She'll stay with you while I go into town for a meeting. I won't be gone long, but you'll be asleep when I get back."

"Be-hee," Abby said in acknowledgment because she knew the teenager—Becky was the sitter Jenna used on special occasions.

"That's right—Becky. She'll read your story tonight, and I'll be sad that I don't get to," Jenna said, bending over to kiss the top of Abby's head and suffering the regret that leaving the child for any reason always caused her.

Abby repositioned herself until she was using the arm Jenna had around her back as a neck brace, resting her head on the sofa cushion and looking up at Jenna with huge, dark brown eyes.

Just gazing down at those chubby pink cheeks, at Abby's perfectly peaked lips, at her cap of blond curls, made Jenna feel as if her heart actually did swell.

"I love you, do you know that?" Jenna said. "I know some awful things brought us together, but I can't help feeling so lucky to have you."

As if she understood that, Abby reached a tiny hand up to smooth Jenna's lightly blushed cheek.

Several years ago, Jenna had hit the point where she wanted kids. A baby. That drive had grown and grown, along with the fear that she wouldn't be allowed to, since every time she'd brought it up with her husband he'd treated the idea as if it were the plague.

The marriage had already been on the downslide by then, and fighting about having a family hadn't helped matters. Then the marriage had ended. And Jenna had wondered—worried—that she might never get to be a mom, to have the child—the children—she had come to so desperately want.

But now she had Abby. And that helped fill so many of the other gaps that had been left in her life.

When she was with Abby like this, she felt some of the peace she was striving for. She felt content. She felt as if everything really would be all right. She felt as if raising Abby, being the best mother she could be to her, was fulfilling enough.

So why did thoughts of Ian Kincaid keep creeping into her mind? Why was she more dressed up than she ordinarily would be for a town meeting and actually looking forward to it? And to having Ian come back here with dinner? Why hadn't she been able to stop reliving that moment when he'd left last night and wondering again and again if he really had been on the verge of kissing her?

She needed to go to the town meeting, but maybe she should tell him that she'd changed her mind about dinner afterwards. Having him repay her for the lasagna wasn't important to her, so maybe she should just cancel with him tonight. She didn't know why she was drawn to him, but resisting it by staying away from him seemed like the smart thing to do. This peace she found alone with Abby was too nice to let anyone else invade it. Maybe years from now she would feel differently. But now was not the time.

"I'll just tell Ian thanks but no thanks for dinner tonight," she muttered.

"Un?" Abby echoed with her form of Ian's name, sounding hopeful.

Jenna laughed again. Apparently Abby did listen when she talked to her. And even when she wasn't talking to her. Plus, it was funny how much the baby liked the man.

"He does seem like a nice guy…." she assured Abby as she stroked the child's head, unreasonably reluctant to call off their after-the-meeting plans. "So, you think it's okay to be friendly with him? Because that's all there is to it—he's just being friendly and I'm just being friendly back. I probably imagined things last night. He probably wasn't going to kiss me…."

Abby sat up quickly and kissed Jenna's cheek as if Jenna had requested that of her.

Again Jenna laughed. "Thank you," she said. "Those are the only kisses I need."

But a purely friendly dinner with Ian tonight after the town meeting?

"That's harmless, isn't it? We both have to eat…." she said in response to her own thoughts.

It *was* harmless, she decided.

Especially if she made sure that she kept her distance when they said good-night, so there wasn't so much as the possibility of a kiss.

Which was exactly what she swore she would do.

And the fact that she'd just talked herself into going through with seeing him again?

Maybe it was better not to think about that.

What Jenna learned at the town meeting was that there still wasn't anywhere near enough money in the Save The Bowen Farm fund to pay her taxes. There was enough to make a bid on the farm at auction, but she was sure that any bid would immediately be topped by the Kincaid Corporation, and that that would be that.

She learned that while the other local farmers were still on her side, she'd lost some support particularly from business owners, due to the mayor's campaign to bring the training facility to Northbridge.

And she learned that Ian was a very persuasive public speaker because even she—who didn't want to hear the merits of bringing the Monarch's training center to town—was enthralled by his speech about the plan's advantages and how the Kincaid Corporation was committed to minimizing any downsides.

Of course she was also enthralled by the sight of him

in another pair of jeans—darker blue than what she'd seen him in before—and a maroon crewneck worn underneath a nearly black sport coat. But he looked so good standing on the stage in the school auditorium that she doubted that she was the only woman there who noticed.

After the meeting, Ian was instantly surrounded by the mayor and the council members. And while Jenna saw him look past them to search the crowd for her, while he kept his eyes on her until she returned the wave he extended, there was no getting near him, so she didn't try.

Instead, after talking with a few friends, she went home, relieved the babysitter, looked in on the soundly sleeping Abby, and then, wondering if Ian might not show up after all, went back downstairs.

She actually wasn't wondering that for long, though, before her doorbell rang, and there he was, bearing two bags from the local general store.

"Those don't look like burgers, Chinese food or pizza," she noted in greeting, leaving him standing on the porch in the still unusually warm weather while she drank in her closer look at him, enjoying it even more than her earlier one at the meeting.

"That's because I didn't bring burgers, Chinese food or pizza," he answered. "I was feeling guilty thinking about what a lousy payback fast food was for the meal you made last night, and I just couldn't do it. I'm not much of a cook, but what I do make is a fantastic sandwich—"

"All humility aside," she goaded him.

"Wait till you taste it," he countered. "The Big Sub—it got me through college, won me friends in high places and women in low places," he said with a wicked smile and a raise of one eyebrow. "It made me famous, in fact. What you will behold in these sacks are the makings for this legendary sandwich."

The man was definitely persuasive. Jenna couldn't suppress a smile at his sales pitch as she pushed open the screen door and let him in.

"*That* is a lot to live up to," she warned.

"Just wait," he said, accepting the challenge as he came in and she closed the door behind him.

He set the bags on the floor, took off his jacket and hung it on one of the coatrack pegs.

"To the kitchen," he said, retrieving the grocery sacks and heading there with Jenna bringing up the rear.

Her gaze rode along on the back pockets of his jeans in admiration of some of the best buns she'd ever seen. It was such an amazing derriere, in fact, that she almost forgot to look up when they reached the kitchen. Ian put the bags on the table and glanced over his shoulder at her. But she did look up, just in the nick of time.

"Here's what I need, and then you can just sit and watch majesty-in-the-making," he was saying. "I need two plates, a bread knife, a paring knife, a fork, a spoon, a cutting board, some salt and a bowl. And something to wipe my hands on."

Jenna gathered his requirements as he emptied the bags. Before sitting at the table, she asked if he wanted something to drink.

"The Big Sub demands beer," he informed her, taking a six-pack of long necks from one of the bags.

"Ah, this really was born in college," she said as she opened two of the already icy-cold bottles.

"Also why glasses are not allowed—it's straight from the bottles or nothing."

Jenna laughed at him, handed him one of the bottles, which he clanked against hers, then held aloft in a silent toast of some sort before he took a swig.

Jenna took a drink of her own beer as she sat at the table next to where he was setting up shop. He began by peeling and slicing a red onion and then dressing it with olive oil, red wine vinegar and the salt that she'd contributed.

She could have easily just watched him, but the silence was awkward, so she said, "How did you get away so soon? I thought the mayor and his minions would have you tied up forever, and even if they let you go, the die-hard football guys were waiting in the wings to nab you."

"Right… Well, I had to promise the die-hard football guys that we'd have a drink and talk as much football as they wanted the next time I ran into them. And the mayor and his minions…" A Cheshire cat grin drew sexy lines at the corners of his eyes. "I told the mayor I had a debt to pay. I was very mysterious, I even winked at him when I said it. I'm pretty sure he thinks I'm doing some under-the-table maneuverings—possibly even paying bribes—to bring the Monarchs here. I didn't have to say much to make him think that I needed to get away to do something he's better off not knowing about—"

"But that he would be in favor of, nonetheless," Jenna contributed wryly.

"He's on the side of the training center," Ian reminded. "But regardless of what he thinks, he made sure I got out of there."

And for that Jenna couldn't help being grateful even though she cautioned herself about not showing it.

"I wasn't sure you'd make it at all," she admitted.

"Why? I told you I would."

"Plans change," Jenna said, recalling her own earlier second thoughts about this.

"I'm a man of my word," Ian declared. "Besides," he added as if he were confiding in her. "I know you and I are probably strange bedfellows, but not only do I like you—and have a really good time whenever I get to see you—I'm thrilled to have something to do in this town that isn't hanging around with couples or talking football—either for business or for the die-hard sports fans."

Jenna's thoughts stuck a little on the bedfellows reference—she had to yank them away from the more literal image the word evoked. Then she had to try to keep his comments about liking her from going to her head in order to concentrate on what he'd gone on to say.

"I mean," he continued, "I'm happy that my brother and sister have partners, but it still seems like everywhere I go around here I'm the fifth wheel. The spare tire. And even though I'm a football fan through and through, too, for me, football talk is still work, and there has to be some time away from it. So believe me, I wouldn't have missed fixing you dinner tonight for anything or anybody."

He said that firmly, convincingly and with a hint of emphasis that put more weight on his wish to be with her than on his desire to escape hanging out with couples or football fanatics.

But again Jenna fought not to take that too seriously

and focused on what he'd said that hadn't had anything to do with her.

"I know all about being the fifth wheel," she said. "There are a *lot* of couples in Northbridge. Everybody is good about including me, but I do always feel like the spare tire when Meg has Logan, and there's Shannon and Dag together and Chase and Hadley. And I could go on and on about the friends I've reconnected with here who are now part of a couple."

And being fresh out of a divorce and finding herself not part of a couple for the first time in ten years made it feel all the more awkward.

"So it's nice," Ian went on, "to come here or see you away from here and have—" he seemed at a loss for how to title what they were doing together "—have your company," was what he settled on.

Jenna also understood the difficulty of categorizing their arrangement. They weren't dating, and to say they were associating with each other socially was a little odd. Certainly she wasn't exactly sure what was going on between them—and she was determined that it was nothing—but that didn't seem to change the fact that she was helpless when it came to denying herself things like last night's dinner or tonight's. So, simply having his *company* seemed like a reasonable explanation. They were just two single people in a town crowded with couples, keeping each other company. Nothing more.

And since that was all there seemed to be to say on the matter, Ian switched gears and said, "Abby's asleep?"

"Since half an hour after I left for the meeting—according to the sitter," Jenna answered as she watched him slice a loaf of crusty Italian bread in half lengthwise, open it up and slather the bottom portion with mayonnaise.

"I brought a bag of mints for us for dessert—believe me, you'll want something to cut the onion taste this sandwich leaves, or you'll hate me by the time you go to bed tonight. But I got a cupcake with a frosting bunny on top for Abby. I figured she would have already had dinner, but I thought she might like a little dessert. You can put it away and give it to her tomorrow."

"She'll love that." And Jenna appreciated that he'd thought of Abby.

For a while they talked about what he was putting on the sandwich as he took the onions out of their marinade and layered them on the mayo-slathered bread. Then he topped them with a variety of lunch meats, then slices of smoked provolone cheese, then more lunch meats, then roasted red peppers, then more lunch meats, tomato, then basil leaves, then fresh mozzarella that he had to slice himself, then salt—

"Salt on lunchmeat?" Jenna protested when she saw him do that.

"No, on the mozzarella—it needs it," he explained.

Then he drizzled some of the oil and vinegar that the onions had been marinating in on the top half of the bread and set it over the fillings.

"That really is a *big* sub," Jenna observed when he had it together.

Ian peered into the grocery bags, then brought out a box of long toothpicks that he stabbed every few inches into the sandwich to hold it together, before he proceeded to slice it.

"I have chips, too," he said as he served her a section,

then took potato chips from the same grocery sack that had held the toothpicks, opened it and put a handful of those on her plate.

He made quick work of cleaning up his preparation mess by scooping all the debris into one of the sacks and leaving the bowl and silverware in the sink. Then, rather than sitting with her, he nodded in the direction of her open back door.

“Want to take advantage of this weird March weather and have a picnic?”

“There isn’t a table or anything out there—it’s all still put away for winter.”

He shrugged an impressive shoulder. “We’ll just prop ourselves against the wall—then it really will be like college,” he said with a smile she just couldn’t say no to.

“This *is* supposed to be the last of the warm temperatures—the news said there’s a cold front coming. So sure, let’s eat outside,” Jenna agreed.

He took the bag of chocolate-covered mint patties out of the second grocery sack, picked up his plate, napkin and beer while Jenna did the same with her place setting and beverage, and they went out the back door.

The house had a beautiful front porch, but in the rear, there was only a utilitarian cement stoop. Ian moved far enough to the right of the back door for both of them to sit there.

And while Jenna was sorry to end up looking out at the yard and the barn rather than at him, it was sort of cozy to be sitting so casually right beside him, up against the warm wall of the house, only inches apart.

She stretched her legs out in front of her and put her plate in her lap.

Ian sat with one thigh against the cement of the stoop, his leg bent and his plate in front of his shin. He braced his arm against his other knee.

"Okay, this lives up to your hype, and I can see how it made you famous in college," Jenna said after her first bite of what was truly a delicious sandwich.

"It can't compare to your lasagna, but as sandwiches go, it's hard to beat," he agreed.

As they settled into the rhythm of eating Jenna said, "From what I gathered tonight—before you persuaded the die-hard football guys to stick to business when they stood up to talk at the meeting—this isn't all you were famous for in college, though. What were all those things they were saying about making your mark in football? About you rivaling your father?"

"I was never a rival to my father," he said with a laugh. "That was actually Hutch. Like I said last night, we both played from the time we were little kids, through high school and college. And we're twins—some people confuse us."

"But you must not have been a *bad* player—I'm sure that would have distinguished you."

"I was a better-than-average player," he conceded. "But I couldn't hold a candle to either my father or Hutch."

"Are you just being modest?" Jenna asked between bites of sandwich and a few potato chips.

"I'm not," he answered after he'd swallowed a mouthful of food and washed it down with some beer. "I tried to be better than I was. I loved playing and I nearly killed myself to make my father proud, not to let him down, not to embarrass him—"

Jenna took a drink of her beer and stole a peek at Ian, seeing again how important pleasing the great Morgan Kincaid had been to him.

"—but Hutch," he was saying, "Hutch had more speed, more natural ability and talent—"

"But you're twins…"

"Identical, right. But we're not the same person. There *are* differences. Plenty of them. And in college, my grade-point average was higher than his, his football stats were higher than mine. So when it came to the pros, I got looked at, talked to, too. But it was Hutch who got the call to play for the NFL."

Jenna looked over at Ian, watching his reaction when she said, "Was that hard for you? Did you resent him for it?"

"Nah," Ian answered easily enough to make her believe he meant it. "I was ready to hit the showers for good and go to work for the Kincaid Corporation. I'd beaten myself up enough trying to be the football star, plus—as careers go—it has a short life span. I thought I could do better things on the business side and that it would actually offer some longevity."

"So did your brother end up playing professionally?"

"He did. For a while. And with a lot of success."

"But he stopped?"

"Yep."

Jenna took the hint—when she asked about other things, Ian was open and forthcoming, but when she touched on the subject of his brother, he clammed up. Clearly he didn't want to talk about his twin.

They'd finished their sandwiches and their beers by

then and after munching a few more chips, Ian tore open the bag of chocolate mint patties.

When he set the candy between them, Jenna took three. "You weren't exaggerating about the sandwich—you deserved to be famous for it. But you were also right about the mints—whew! Those onions were delicious but potent!"

"I'm glad you liked it," he said more humbly now as he unwrapped a mint patty for himself, too.

"So you didn't want to talk football tonight, and I ended up making you sort of do it anyway—sorry about that," Jenna said then. "I'm as bad as the die-hard fans."

He set his plate to the side and pivoted somewhat away from the wall, angling more toward her and flashing her a devilish smile. "Are you a fan?"

"Of football? Is that the one with the round balls or the pinched-off oval ball?" she joked to let him know she was not well-versed in any sport.

He laughed. "Actually, I was *not* asking if you were a fan of football…."

"Ohhh, you want to know if I'm a fan of *yours*…." she said, as if she hadn't known that was what he was teasing her about all along. "Well, you do make a fine sandwich and I like the mints," she added, popping her third one into her mouth to finally obliterate the onion taste.

"But me, you can take or leave?" he persisted.

"You're not so bad…" was all she would allow him, unable to suppress a smile at the fun of giving him a hard time.

"Because I was thinking," he said then, "Meg said you were coming to the Bruiser's basketball game with her and Logan tomorrow night—that means more couples and you and I. Then there's that dance on Friday night, the rehearsal dinner for Shannon and Dag's wedding on Saturday night, the wedding on Sunday—couples, couples, couples, and you and I…"

"Uh-huh…" she agreed, wondering where he was going with this.

"I know we only agreed not to avoid each other, to maybe have a glass of wine together when we're in the same place at the same time, but I was thinking that if I could lock you in for all of these things coming up, I might look forward to them a little more than I have been."

"Oh, now that *does* sound appealing—lock me in? Will there be handcuffs? An ankle bracelet?"

He laughed. "I'm okay with either of those if you are," he countered suggestively.

Then he said, "All kidding aside—though that *is* one of the reasons I have a good time with you—could we *keep each other company* through those events? Or would you rather be the spare tire on the women's side and make me be the spare tire on the guys'?"

Which Jenna knew was exactly the way it would play out.

And she was definitely tiring of being the one sitting with a forced smile on her face while the couples around her whispered or snuggled or shared a private joke that she pretended to get but didn't.

If she took Ian up on his offer, at those moments she would at least have him to talk to.

"We'd be keeping each other company as friends, right?" she asked.

"As friends," he confirmed. "We'll call ourselves Spare Tires United."

"I'm not wearing a button that says that," she warned, again joking.

"You can keep it in your purse, take it out only as necessary—like a badge."

It was nice that they shared the same sense of humor....

"Okay then..." Jenna finally agreed, though not wholeheartedly because to unleash the full spectrum of how happy it made her to think of being "locked in" to sharing the next three events with him seemed dangerous. They were only doing this as a convenience, she insisted to herself. Joining forces as the odd ones out.

"Great! Then we're on!" he said enthusiastically to her lukewarm concession.

A sudden shiver shook Jenna. She'd been so interested in Ian that she hadn't realized that the temperature had dropped and that it was getting much cooler than it had been when they'd first brought their dinner outside.

"Feels like the cold snap is coming right on schedule," she said.

"And I should probably take off," Ian added, getting to his feet and holding out a hand to help her up, too.

It would have been rude not to accept the assistance, so she did, fighting not to be aware of the feel of his hand closing around hers or the strength in it or how much she liked it.

The moment she was up and steady, she slipped out of his grip. Because she really was determined that this be nothing....

They gathered their plates and the bag of mints—each of them having one more as they went inside. Jenna assured Ian that she would take care of the little that remained to be cleaned. Then she followed him to the front door.

She had no idea why she was itching to hold his jacket for him to slip on, but she was. She managed to keep herself from doing anything like that, however, by putting her hands into the pockets of her slacks while he got his coat on all by himself.

Then he moved nearer to the door, put one hand on the knob and turned to her as she said, "Thanks for dinner—it really was the best sandwich I've ever eaten, and I'm glad I got to watch you put it together, so I can make it again myself."

"Damn! I didn't realize I'd be revealing my secrets!"

"Sorry, but it's too late—I know them all now," she answered to his joke.

He smiled a too-sexy-to-believe smile and said, "Maybe not *all* of them."

"Oh, right, I don't want to blow your mystery-man image...."

That made his smile stretch into a grin as he looked more intently at her, studied her face, her eyes.

"Yep, you've changed my whole perspective about going to the stuff coming up," he said after a moment, his voice quiet. "Thanks for that."

Without warning, he dipped forward and kissed her.

On the mouth, but he was there and gone so quickly that it was almost as if it hadn't happened at all. Except for the slight tingling left on her lips.

Jenna felt her forehead wrinkle into quizzical lines as the shock of that kiss, and the disappointment of not having had the chance to actually feel it, washed over her.

Ian must have noticed, because he laughed slightly and then made a return trip to kiss her brow—lingering enough this time so the warmth of his breath, the softness of his lips made an impression. Just not where she wanted them to…

Then he straightened up, said a simple, "See you tomorrow night," and left.

A couple of little pecks goodnight. Between two people who are becoming friends....

Neither of those kisses had meant anything more—that was what Jenna told herself as she watched Ian go out to his car, get in and drive away.

And she couldn't have stopped the kisses, because she hadn't seen either of them coming, she reasoned. Which she would have done if she had, she told herself, in keeping with her earlier vow that no good-night kissing, or even the thought of good-night kissing, was allowed tonight.

Yet as she closed the door, it wasn't so much stopping the kisses that was still on her mind.

Instead, she kept recalling the sensation of having Ian kiss her forehead and imagining that same sensation on lips that were hungering for him.

Hungering for more than a kiss that was just a little peck between two friends.

And who was she really kidding? she asked herself.

Because if he *had* given her a kiss that was more than a little peck between friends there was no way she would have put a stop to it….

Chapter Six

The unusually warm March weather ended overnight, and on Thursday, late-winter temperatures returned with three inches of heavy, wet snow. It wasn't near enough to slow things down in Northbridge, day or night, however. So the Bruisers—the local men's sports team that pitted brothers and old friends against each other in whatever sport was in season—still played basketball that evening in the high-school gym.

The weekly games were all in good fun and always drew a large crowd, most of which went from the game straight to Adz, the town's most popular restaurant and bar. Adz was so popular that it had recently expanded for the second time, taking over an additional storefront and making it a game room.

The pool table that had been added during the first expansion was moved into the game room and joined by a foosball table, a Ping-Pong table, an air-hockey game, two pinball tables, a Skee-Ball section and a wall that offered darts and another game call Ringing the Bull. There were also video games, penny-pitching games and a bookcase filled with board games that included checkers and chess.

While Ian had sat beside Jenna at the Bruisers' basketball game, when they'd arrived with everyone else at Adz, it had been impossible for them to stick together.

The die-hard football fans spotted Ian the minute they walked in and demanded that he make good on his promise of the previous night to have a drink with them and talk football. And as one of the few medical professionals in Northbridge, it was difficult for Jenna to go anywhere and not meet a barrage of health questions.

It wasn't until Ian broke away from the football fans and inched Jenna into the game room that they could finally spend some time together. And even then they were only left alone if they played the games.

Not that Jenna minded. In fact she had a lot of fun. She ordinarily didn't have anyone to play with.

"What's the score?" Ian demanded after she beat him shooting pool.

"I'm three for three here," she said, not shy about her victories.

"But I was three for three at air hockey," Ian reminded her.

"We tied at foosball. I won one more at pinball—"

"But I cleaned your clock at Ping-Pong," Ian boasted with relish.

"You only beat me by two, and I had better aim at darts—where I cleaned *your* clock! And then there was Ringing The Bull…."

Ringing The Bull was a game in which a genuine bull's nose ring attached to a string was tossed by the string to hook onto a bull's horn mounted on the wall.

Ian laughed. "Yeah, how is it that you're so good at that?"

Jenna had no idea, but she wasn't about to admit it. "I believe it's pure talent," she said with a heavy dose of mock superiority.

"Uh-huh," Ian said dubiously, laughing again. "And then there's Skee-Ball..." he added, taking his turn at goading. "If I'm remembering right, that made us about even. What do you want to do to break the tie?"

He said that with some salaciousness to his tone, and Jenna shook her head at him as if he were incorrigible. But all evening, their game playing had been full of the teasing and joking that they were both so quick with, and tonight it had more of a note of flirting to it than previously.

It was more fun than Jenna had had in a very long time.

Of course, it also hadn't hurt that she'd had the opportunity to steal innumerable glances at Ian's divine derriere in the jeans he was wearing. Or that she'd had the chance to watch his back, his shoulders, his muscular chest in action beneath his bulky fisherman's knit sweater. Or that his hair had just the right amount of dishevel to it tonight and his handsome face was showing a hint of beard. Altogether, he looked ruggedly masculine with just a bit of scraggly charm.

Still, before deciding what they should do to break their tie, she asked a passing waitress what time it was. The answer nixed any further fun and games.

"I need to get home," she said.

"You said you put Abby to bed before you left tonight. The sitter is just sitting—"

"But it's a school night for my sitter and I promised I'd be back by eleven—it's that now."

"So we just agree that we are worthy adversaries and save true conquest for another day."

Jenna laughed at his melodramatic declaration. "Was one of us going to conquer the other?" she inquired with her own hint of insinuation.

Ian did nothing but wiggle his eyebrows up and down in answer to that.

Then he said, "Okay, home it is," and Jenna appreciated how good-naturedly he was taking her need to call such an abrupt halt to their fun.

Getting out of Adz was no quick-and-easy task. Good-nights had to be said along the way, the football fans tried to nab Ian again, and Jenna's medical expertise was called upon by three more people.

But eventually, they made it to the coatrack and donned their coats before slipping out into the cold March air to Ian's sedan, parked a few slots from the door.

"It's so quiet." Ian marveled at the difference between the noise of Adz and the silence of a deserted Main Street.

"Quiet and pretty, isn't it?" Jenna chimed in, gazing at the dusting of snow that glistened in the glow of the wrought-iron streetlights that lined the wide avenue. "It's almost pretty enough to stall my spring fever."

"But not quite," Ian guessed as he unlocked the passenger door of his car and opened it for her.

"No, I'm ready for spring," Jenna conceded as she got in.

Once she was securely inside, Ian closed the door, and Jenna watched him round the front of the Mercedes. He'd put on a peacoat over his sweater, and it had just added to his rugged appeal. So much so that she wasn't sure if the shiver that rippled through her just then was in response to the cold seeping in through her own jeans, turtleneck sweater and wool coat, or if it was a reaction to just how good he looked.

She tried to tell herself that it was the former and kept her eyes straight ahead as he got behind the wheel and started the car.

"Sooo," he said, "nurses don't get to leave their jobs at the office either—if tonight was any indication."

Jenna shrugged that off with a smile. "No, not usually. Especially in Northbridge, where everybody knows me."

"And they come to you with the kind of stuff I'd see a doctor for. Even after hours, in a bar, when you're socializing."

"People are less shy when they're worried about some health issue. It's okay, it comes with the territory."

"It's okay to have some beefy guy pull up his pant leg to show you a boil just when you've taken a sip of your hot, buttered rum?" Ian asked with some squeamishness that amused Jenna.

"Don't tell me you didn't see yucky stuff on the football field—broken bones, dislocated shoulders, bloody noses, cuts and scrapes. 'Fess up—you were the team fainter," she teased him.

Ian laughed. "As if that wouldn't have made all the

papers—'Son of football legend Morgan Kincaid faints at the sight of blood,'" he said as if he were reading headlines. Then he added, "I can take my fair share. But I never had to have some guy's blood and guts spilled on me while I'm eating French fries dipped in ketchup and drinking foamy drinks. You can't tell me it isn't unappetizing."

Jenna looked over at him and grinned, relishing the sight of his profile. "I can take it," she said, as if the stamina for gore was yet another thing they were competing about.

Ian kept his eyes on the road and smiled. "Oh, I get it—*this* is the tie-breaker. Okay, fine, you win," he conceded, as if it were no concession at all.

But it delighted Jenna that they were so much on the same wavelength that he'd known what she was doing and gotten the joke, so she let him off the hook and returned to what had gotten them there in the first place—talk of people accessing her medical services tonight.

"It's no big deal that I get asked health questions everywhere I go. I don't mind."

"Then there was that last woman," Ian said, easily switching back to their previous subject, too. "The one who asked you to feel the lump on her husband's neck—what was that comment she made about what a shame it was that you didn't become a doctor? About how she'd never get over it?"

"That was my old high-school chemistry teacher," Jenna explained. "Being a doctor was what I planned to be way back when, and she knew it. Encouraged it. Did everything she could to help me. That was what she was talking about."

"Really? You wanted to be a doctor?" Ian said, intrigued.

"Oh, yeah. From the time I was a little kid."

"When you got a doctor's kit for Christmas?"

"I *asked* for a doctor's kit for Christmas," she amended.

"Then you *seriously* wanted to be a doctor? Even as a kid?"

"I did. Like you playing Little League football—it started that early for me, too. Except it was my own idea, not something someone else wanted for me. I even shadowed the local doctor who was here then. He was just an old-fashioned country doctor, before progress came to Northbridge, and he took me under his wing. I'd go to his office after school and on Saturdays—because yes, he worked Saturdays, too—and follow him around. And do a few things here and there."

"You practiced medicine without a license? As a *kid?*" Ian teased her.

"Mostly I just watched and listened—if the patient was willing, of course. But as I got older, I got to take out stitches, change dressings, write down histories—simple stuff that still gave me a little experience. Plus, by the time I was a teenager, I did some of the home-care visits that didn't really require more than looking in on recuperating patients, making sure their wounds were healing, that they were taking their medications, that they were doing all right."

Ian did take his eyes off the road then to glance at her. "That was your after-school job?"

"Oh, I didn't get paid. I just did it. I babysat in the evenings to make money."

"So, the woman tonight who said you should have become a doctor knew what she was talking about."

"Mrs. Williams. She knew how much I wanted that. I took all of her classes along with every other science class that I could take, and she even got me into a special program my senior year that let me cross over to the college for some higher-level chem classes and an anatomy course."

"As a high-school kid you took college classes—that were basically pre-med—to get a leg up on going to medical school? You had to have been pretty sharp, too."

That embarrassed Jenna. "I did okay," was all she said.

"That's what I call focused. But then you became a nurse instead?"

"Right."

"How did that happen? Did you change your mind? Not get into any medical school anywhere? I know that can be nearly impossible…."

Jenna gauged how much she wanted to tell him and then gave him only the thumbnail version. "I set aside my goals for someone else."

"A guy?" Ian guessed.

"A guy. Love. Marriage. You know—*that* stuff," she confirmed, trying to make light of it. "But it isn't as if I don't like being a nurse. I do. I love it, in fact."

"Still, it isn't the same, and if being a doctor was what you wanted—"

"No, it isn't the same. But in a lot of ways I prefer the position I'm in as a nurse. People don't put me on the same kind of pedestal they put doctors on, so they feel more free with me, more open. There's a different connection, and I like that."

"So, no regrets?"

"Oh, there are lots of those," Jenna answered with a laugh.

Ian took his eyes off the road a second time to give her a more somber look. "All kidding aside—do you have regrets?"

"If I knew then what I know now? Would I have made the same choices, the same sacrifices?"

"Yeah...."

"I think I would have done things differently, yes. But it's water under the bridge."

The man was even terrific-looking when he frowned—which he did before he turned his eyes back to the road.

"Have you thought about going to medical school now?" Ian asked after a moment.

She thought it disturbed him to know she had regrets.

"I actually did think about it," Jenna assured him. "But I'm at a different stage of my life now, I want different things, and—"

"Abby?" he made another guess.

"Abby, sure. But even before Abby—somewhere along the way I became less of a science geek and more of a caregiver," she said. "The shift happened about the same time that I started to want kids."

"Which was when?"

"About three years ago."

"So, completely before Abby?"

"Yeah. I wanted kids of my own. I realized I was ready to have them."

"But…" Ian prompted carefully, as if he thought he might be treading on painful ground.

"That was complicated. Not physically, just… It wasn't something my husband and I agreed on," she said. Which was more than she wanted to say.

Ian must have gotten that message because he didn't press further and instead continued with what they'd been talking about. "So you started to want kids a while ago, then things here fell apart more recently and…"

"And after my marriage ended I considered medical school again, but putting my energies into my personal life was more what I wanted to do, so I decided against it. Then—boom! My mom had the heart attack, I came home and discovered things had fallen apart and…" She shrugged. "I ended up adopting Abby. But I adopted Abby because I wanted Abby. Not going to medical school now is not because of Abby."

"Okay, I think I get all that. But still you have regrets…."

Jenna laughed. "Don't you?"

He seemed to consider that for a moment before he said, "I've made mistakes—that's for sure. But I think I've learned some valuable lessons from them, so to say that I have regrets? Or would do something differently if I knew then what I know now? I don't think so."

"Well, trust me, you learn from the things you end up regretting, too," Jenna concluded. And she was tired of talking about herself, so she turned the tables and said, "What about those mistakes you made? Were they professional or personal or—"

"Overlap," he answered confusing her and fueling her

curiosity. He took a right onto the road that led to her house. Then pulled to a stop next to her babysitter's car.

Rather than persuading him to clarify right at that moment, she said, "Do you want to come in?"

"I really do," he said. "But I also know that you have a six a.m. shift tomorrow, and it's already nearly midnight."

He'd listened when she'd talked to Meg about bringing Abby over at dawn, *and* he was being considerate.

Why couldn't he do something—anything—that she could find fault with?

Despite her early morning schedule, she was still disappointed that this was the end of her time with him.

"I'll walk you up, though," he said as he put the car in park and got out.

Jenna opened her own door, but Ian was there the minute she did, holding it to make sure it stayed open while she got out.

It occurred to her as they went up the porch steps that it might have been better if he hadn't walked her to her front door. Because that was when she started thinking about good-night kisses again. About the one that had been so hit-and-run that she'd hardly registered it. And the one that had only happened on her forehead.

Not tonight, she swore. Not at all. *Not in any way, shape or form....*

She was determined not to set herself up for any of that tonight. She wasn't even going to look at him when she said good-night.

Except that he made that a little difficult when he reached the door ahead of her and stood in her way, his back to the house, looking at her.

Studying her, in fact. And making it impossible for her not to elevate her gaze to that stunningly attractive face dusted in porch light.

When he knew he had her attention, he smiled down at her. A small, ruminative smile.

"You know," he finally said, "I've been to two of the Bruisers' games on my other visits here. And ended up at Adz with everyone else. But I have to say that tonight was the best time I've ever had doing that."

She felt the same way. But she didn't want to let on, so she merely said, "I'm glad. Of course it helps that the Bruisers won…."

Ian laughed. "They're all Bruisers, they just divide up and play each other—they can't lose."

Again, it was nice that he got her jokes.

"I don't remember seeing you at other Bruisers' games," she said. She had no doubt that she would have noticed him.

"Maybe you were working," he suggested.

Or taking care of her father or Abby or not in the mood to socialize after her dad's death. Admittedly, she hadn't gone to many games since then. Or had too many nights out. But it seemed simpler to just agree. "Probably."

Ian went on studying her for another moment before he said, "I'm just glad you weren't working tonight. Or tomorrow night for the dance and then the rehearsal dinner and the wedding," he added, his voice quieter. "Looks like I'm in luck this trip."

Then he brought a big hand to the side of her face cupping its contours and tilting it up to look more intently into her eyes.

"I think I like you more than I should...." he said in an almost-whisper that didn't sound as if it was meant for her to hear.

And with that he leaned in and kissed her again, taking her mouth gently at first, causing her to think he was going to make a quick getaway—like he had the night before.

But he didn't do that. Instead, the kiss went on long enough for her to get comfortable with it.

Long enough for her to remind herself that she shouldn't be allowing him to kiss her at all, to tell herself that she should stop it, and instead to kiss him back.

So easily, so naturally that it almost shocked her to think that Ian was the first man she'd kissed since she'd met her ex-husband. *Really* kissed, so that it counted.

But oh, boy, did this one count!

He deepened the kiss then, parting his lips.

Jenna's lips parted, too. He gently massaged her cheek as her own hand found its way to his chest. His rock-hard chest that had way, way too many layers of clothing covering it.

Still, she could feel the solidity of him even through the thick sweater, through his jacket, while the kiss went on and on, giving her the chance to savor the suppleness of his mouth, the sweet taste of him, the sense of contained power and strength that emanated from him.

She lost herself in that kiss so completely that tonight the surprise was when it came to an end.

A slow, lingering end that said he wasn't any more eager for that than she was. But an end nonetheless.

And when it had, he again peered into her eyes.

His brows arched as if he were as dazed by the potency of that kiss as she had been.

Jenna couldn't find words for what had just happened between them, and apparently neither could Ian, because all he did was whisper, "I'll see you tomorrow night," before he took his hand from her face, stepped away from her and went back to his car.

But Jenna couldn't make herself move just yet. She stayed in the cold, watching him go, reliving that kiss in her mind while the feel of it was still on her mouth.

And letting the chilly air cool the heat of her cheeks before she had to face the babysitter.

Who, with any luck, wouldn't be able to tell that inside Jenna was all churned up and wishing, wishing, wishing that that kiss was still going on…

And thinking that whoever Chelsea was, she should be sorry all she was getting from Ian Kincaid was a playlist….

Chapter Seven

"Calm down, Dad," Ian said to his father the next evening as he was getting dressed for the Spring Fling Dance.

Morgan Kincaid was in a huff on the other end of the cell phone.

"How did you even know Chelsea had called?" Ian asked after his father had read him the riot act.

"I had drinks with her father late this afternoon, that's how. He told me to convey the message to you that Chelsea was leaving today for a photo shoot in the country where she won't be reachable. Where she'll be for the next two weeks! Two weeks that you won't be able to even talk to her, and you didn't answer when she called this morning or call her back!"

Morgan Kincaid had not calmed down.

Ian hadn't expected his father to know about the call

from Chelsea, but he refused to be ruffled by the fact that he did.

"The time difference is a problem—Paris is eight hours ahead of us, you know. I was in a breakfast meeting when the call came in, so it went to voicemail. She had already left Paris and was unreachable when I finally listened to the message—"

"And now *two weeks* will go by without you being able to talk to her!"

"Dad! This is not worth stroking out over. It was a missed phone call. No big deal. She was only calling to give me a heads-up on a new musician she discovered, and she left the message on my voicemail. I'm going to say it again—Chelsea and I are nothing—*nothing*—but friendly." Ian said each of those words slowly, precisely, emphatically. "We are not an item. Or a couple. Or anything. *Friendly*—that's it."

"You need to fix that!"

"There's nothing to fix. If not for the connection between you and her father, and the connection you want between the Monarchs and Tanner Brewery, she and I probably wouldn't even be friends. Missing a call from her certainly wouldn't be and isn't a crisis. And whether or not you want to believe it, it isn't a crisis on Chelsea's side, either—so I didn't talk to her? So what?"

"So what? So this is important! Sponsorship from her father is important—"

"Which I will likely get us with or without Chelsea—I told you that, too. I spoke to Bill Tanner yesterday and he's seeing the advantages of backing the Monarchs. I assured him that I'm also urging Chelsea to do the ad campaign but I made no promises—"

"Maybe you should have. Maybe he'd be signed on already if you had."

"What should I have promised? To marry his daughter and keep her barefoot and pregnant so he could see her every day?" Ian said facetiously. "Because none of that is going to happen. I'm not going to get into anything with this woman because you *or* her father might like it if I did! This is business and that's as far as it goes. And if that's a deal breaker with Tanner Brewery, then that's the way it is."

"You need to give this the full-court press!" his father still insisted.

"It's her father and his business that I'm giving the full-court press. And I'll get this endorsement like I get every other endorsement—through hard work and diligence and salesmanship. Remember that we learned this lesson the hard way—mix business, family and romance, and it all goes bad. All of it. We'll get Tanner Brewery as a sponsor, I'll do what I can to get Chelsea to be the face of our new partnership to please her father, but we'll do it by the book."

"It still doesn't help to miss her calls," Morgan persisted.

"It also doesn't hurt anything," Ian said, standing his ground.

He heard his father's sigh on the other end of the line but Morgan let the subject drop. They discussed a few details about the training center and then Ian brought the call to a close. But after he'd hung up he did feel a twinge of guilt for lying to his father.

He hadn't had a breakfast meeting this morning.

When Chelsea had called he could have answered.

He just hadn't wanted to.

He'd been awake, lying in bed, thinking about Jenna. About having kissed her the night before. And the last thing he'd wanted to do at that moment was talk to another woman, even if it *had* only been about music. And even if, for the sake of business, he probably should have.

As he chose a black cashmere turtleneck sweater to wear tonight with his dark gray slacks, his thoughts turned to last night.

Oh, yeah, he'd been thinking about that kiss all right....

Whew!

Last night had been a kiss!

Jenna was something...

She was great. Sweet and beautiful and smart and quick and funny. What red-blooded man wouldn't have wanted to kiss her?

Still, he shouldn't have. And not because of Chelsea—Chelsea was a nonissue no matter what his father or hers might want. He shouldn't have kissed Jenna because of Abby.

Because when it came to big deals, Jenna having Abby was one of them.

He wasn't ready for diapers and feedings and naptimes and bedtimes and babysitters and thinking and worrying and taking care of a kid. Living a life that revolved around a kid. The way Jenna did.

Someday he would be. But he wasn't ready for it now.

And more importantly, when he was ready for it, he really, really wanted the kid to be his own.

He respected and admired Jenna for taking on Abby. But when he had kids himself, he wanted the full experience. He'd heard friends talk about how there was nothing like having their newborn handed to them. That there was nothing like the feelings that had washed over them when they'd looked down at the little being of their own making. When they saw themselves or the people they loved in their child's face or mannerisms.

And he wanted to know what that was like. He wanted that bonding-at-birth experience for his own sake and for the sake of any child whose life he touched. That bonding-at-birth experience that he obviously hadn't had with his father.

That bonding-at-birth experience that might have made him feel differently….

Not that he hadn't loved his mother, that he didn't love his father, he thought as he pulled on his pants.

Not that he wasn't grateful for everything they'd done for him, given him. He was.

And not that they hadn't been and weren't his parents because they *were* the only parents he'd ever truly known. Parents he would have and still would do anything for, his parents to the end.

It was just that he didn't want any child of his to have the lifelong sense he'd had that he needed to work harder to be worthy of those parents because the child hadn't been born to him.

In the grand scheme of his own life, he wanted things to be strictly traditional—meet the right girl, fall in love, be alone together for a while, make the decision to have kids when they were both ready for it, create those kids, have and raise those kids together. He wanted the kind of closeness to those kids that came from that kind of irrefutable, undeniable, unbreakable connection.

Jenna could well have something close to that with Abby, because while she wasn't Abby's biological mother, she was still family. Blood. They were still connected.

But him? If anything developed between himself and Jenna, if he ended up a fixture in Abby's life? It wouldn't be the same with him.

And it sure as hell wouldn't fit that traditional picture he had of himself, of his future, of his life.

No, being with Jenna wouldn't fit his game plan at all, he thought as he shrugged into the sweater and peered into the mirror over the sink.

"So don't go around kissing her," he told his reflection when he picked up his brush to straighten out his hair.

Yeah, kissing was a bad move.

"That has to stop. Here and now," he ordered his reflected image. "Keeping each other company with the couples—that's all there can be to this. Back off the personal stuff. And don't kiss her again!"

He knew that was exactly how he should play it. Just friends. That's what they'd agreed to. That's what he needed to stick to.

But then he thought about dancing with her tonight. Holding her in his arms even with other people around. About how talking to her came so easily. About how quick-witted she was and how she always made him laugh, always kept him on his toes. About how the minute he set eyes on her, everything around them, everyone around them, faded into the background and all he could see, all he could think about, was her.

And he knew he was going to want to kiss her again….

"Just don't!" he told himself as if he and his reflection were two separate entities.

But as he stepped away from the mirror he honestly didn't know if he could resist….

By the last dance of the Spring Fling, Jenna had been spun, twirled, dipped and turned every which way. She'd long ago freed her feet from the pain of shoes that hadn't ever seen that much action, pushed up the sleeves of her handmade boatneck sweater with its crocheted hem and wished she'd worn a skirt instead of slacks. She should have realized that attending a function like this with someone who not only knew how to dance, but who was also an athlete, would keep her on her toes.

But it *was* the last dance—thankfully, a slow one—in the candlelit church basement adorned with multicolored wild flowers both real and in the form of paper streamers to give the feel of Spring. And Ian was holding her just close enough for her to look up at his sculpted face as they did little more than merely sway to the music.

"Okay, I really have to know," she said in reference to something Ian had artfully dodged all evening, "how does Super-Jock-The-Football-Star dance like you've danced tonight? And no fooling around this time."

When he broke out the devilish smile, she knew she was weaponless against him if he did joke his way around giving a serious answer.

But he obliged her, "That was my mother's input. She was afraid my father was making Hutch and I into grunting gorillas who couldn't do anything but play football. She wanted us to have some culture and refinement, too—that's what she said. When we were kids she tried to take us to the opera, the ballet, but we just embarrassed her by being two rowdy boys who fought with each other over the armrest, laughed at the men in tights, made fun of—"

"In other words, you were gorillas."

"Pretty much. Then she sold my dad on dance lessons the year before she died. She said that because dance was physical and about movement, it could help us on the football field, make us more agile, help our response time, things along those lines. And once Dad looked at it like that, he got behind it and—"

"Pushed you to excel at it, so you learned to be good dancers."

"And kept it up even after Mom was gone. He also assured us—out of earshot of my mother—that it would help us get girls." The devilish smile grew more devilish. "And he was right."

Jenna did not believe that Ian had ever had any problem getting girls, whether or not he could dance. But it was nice that he knew how to dance, although he'd nearly danced her to death—no exercise class, no double shift at any hospital, no hike, jog or farm work, no marathon shopping trip had ever worn her out as much as he had.

Which was why, she told herself, she was so pliant in his arms. Why she was longing for him to hold her closer, tighter. Why she wanted to just mold herself to him and rest her head on his chest.

It was all merely the weariness. It had nothing to do

with the fact that she might be longing to be held closer and tighter, to be molded up against him with her head on his chest.

"Well, I'm not sure who to thank, but I've never danced as much as I've danced tonight, and it was nice not sitting on the sidelines, watching everyone else dance for a change."

"The ex didn't dance?" Ian asked.

"Nooo. No way. Never," she said. "He *hated* it."

That seemed to prompt Ian to tighten his arm around her the way she'd been wishing he would. He pulled her just a bit closer.

She moved her hand on his back in response and closed the separation between them a hint more.

"Well, I'm glad we got to do this tonight," Ian said, dropping his chin to the top of Jenna's head.

And what could she do when that happened? She couldn't just stiffen her neck as if she were providing some sort of pedestal for him. The natural thing was for her to turn her head to the side and lay her cheek to his cashmere-clad chest.

At least that's what felt like the natural thing to do when she did it.

Natural and so, so nice…

And not noticeably out of the ordinary since everyone around them was dancing basically the same way to the very slow music that the band was playing.

Unfortunately, after only a few minutes the music drew to an end, and everyone stopped dancing—including Jenna and Ian. Jenna had had only the briefest taste of that nearness she'd been craving. A teaser of how nice it actually could be—and was—before it was gone and they weren't even touching any longer.

But Jenna bucked up, told herself it shouldn't have happened in the first place and clapped along with everyone else. People shouted thanks and praise for the band whose members took a bow, then turned to pack away their instruments, signaling that the evening had really and truly come to an end.

The crowd had dwindled considerably since the Spring Fling started. So after slipping her feet back into her shoes, Jenna and Ian had an easy time making their way to the door where the last of the revelers were putting on coats.

Saying good-night to everyone didn't take too long, and then Jenna was in the passenger seat of Ian's car again as he rounded the front end and slid behind the wheel.

The drive home was quick, and Ian insisted on coming inside with her to pay her babysitter tonight. Not that Jenna minded that he came in—she'd been wondering if she should invite him, telling herself she shouldn't and still trying to find a good reason to do it.

And once he was inside, had paid the sitter and it was just the two of them again, Jenna offered him a nightcap. Just to be polite, of course. Which Ian accepted—probably for the same reason, she thought.

Ian took off his jacket and hung it on the coatrack while Jenna poured some of her father's brandy in two juice glasses—apologizing for the fact that she didn't have brandy snifters—and then they went into the living room to sit on her sofa.

Jenna kicked off her shoes, making sure to hug one

end of the couch when she sat down. But Ian sat in the center. And since they were angled to face each other, there was not quite as much distance between them as there might have been. As there should have been.

"Are you working at all this weekend?" Ian asked her, settling in with an arm braced atop the sofa back after his first sip of brandy.

"No, I have the whole weekend off. Do you?" she asked.

"I have some paperwork to do, some emails that need sending, a few phone calls—"

"Your-Father-The-Boss is making you work on the weekend?" Jenna teased him.

Ian smiled an indulgent smile. "You know, to everyone *except* my father, *I'm* the boss."

"What exactly are you?"

"I'm the Chief Operating Officer of the Monarchs football team."

"But you still work for your father."

Ian rolled his eyes. "I work for my father, and everyone else works for me."

"Have you always worked for your father? I know you said you went from college to the Kincaid Corporation, so—"

"Actually," Ian said, swirling his brandy and watching it coat the glass, "no, I haven't always worked for my father."

"Really..." Jenna said, surprised and intrigued.

"Mmm. About six years ago I left the family business."

"That's as long as it's been since you saw your brother, isn't it?"

Ian raised his glass in toast. "Good memory."

"Why did you leave the family business?" Jenna asked then, knowing she was prying. Sitting there so cozily drinking brandy, bone tired from working all day and dancing like mad all evening, she somehow didn't have as many qualms about being nosy.

"There was some family drama and some fallout from it," he said.

But that was all he offered. Jenna sipped her own brandy, hoping her silence might get him to say more.

Instead, he went on talking about the path his career had been on, which was what she'd asked about in the first place. "That was before we got the NFL franchise. There was an opening in the head office of a floundering football team in Arizona. I was more than happy to switch from corporate business to the business end of football, so I took the job, lived in Phoenix for three years. And between me on the business end and a new coaching staff on the field, we put that team back on the map."

Jenna could see that he was proud of the accomplishment and raised her glass to clink against his in congratulations.

Then she said, "So you were your own man for a while, and then you went back to doing your father's bidding?"

He laughed. "I've always been my own man. That isn't something Hutch or I ever had a problem with, despite being twins, despite how much our father was involved in our lives—that's what's *caused* problems among the three of us."

But he still didn't explain what those problems were.

"And we all do the *bidding* of whomever is paying our salary," he went on. "The fact that that person is my father is just a coincidence. I'm good at what I do—which I proved in Arizona—and I get offers all the time trying to lure me away from the Kincaid Corporation and now the Monarchs. If I wanted to, I could walk out tomorrow and pick and choose from half a dozen jobs—which is what I did six years ago."

"And then you came back…."

"It's family. We patched things up. And I wouldn't pass up the chance to start from scratch with an expansion team like the Monarchs even if I didn't have a personal interest in it."

"But it meant going back to work for your father…."

He laughed again. "You're really stuck on that, aren't you? To tell you the truth, I actually have more freedom to say no to my father when I don't agree with him *because* he's my father. And I've never thought of my job as 'doing his bidding.' It isn't as if I'm his henchman or something. Even right this minute, when he's fine buying this property at auction, if you said you'd sell to us but at a premium price, I could and would put a check in your hand tomorrow."

"Because you don't want the Monarchs to look bad. And since neither does your father—"

"I'd put a big, fat check in your hand tomorrow, because I hate seeing you come up on the short end of this when you don't have to."

"But I do," she said stubbornly.

"Because your dad got you to promise to do whatever you could to keep his farm a farm—so now which one of us is really doing their father's bidding?"

Jenna clinked glasses with him a second time, conceding that he had a point. Then they both finished their brandies and set the glasses on the coffee table.

"Now tell me I was also right about tonight," he commanded. "It was sooo much better to be there together and not as the stand-ins when one part of a couple needed to sit out a dance."

"Is this a roundabout way of asking me if I had a good time tonight?" she challenged.

The mischief in his smile was answer enough, but still he said, "Did you?"

"I did. But I already told you that it was nice not sitting on the sidelines, watching everyone else dance," Jenna said, in weariness letting her head fall back against the sofa cushion.

She'd twisted her hair into a French knot and left a geyser of waves at her crown, and while she hadn't intended for that geyser of waves to hit his hand, they apparently did, because he began to toy with them.

"I know that's what you told me," he said quietly. "I just wanted to be sure you had fun."

"Well, I did. Did you?"

"Oh, yeah…." he said with a contented-cat smile as his gaze caressed her face. "Always…." he added in a near whisper.

Then he leaned far enough forward that Jenna had only to tilt her head slightly away from the couch cushion to accommodate his mouth meeting hers.

Fleetingly, it occurred to her that they shouldn't be kissing again. But maybe she was just too tired to pay attention to that mental nay-saying, because all she could really focus on was the feel of his warm, supple lips parting over hers. And all she could manage to do was part her own lips in response and return that slow, languorous kiss, savoring it, savoring the warmth of him, the mingling of his brandied breath with her own, the talent he had for more than dancing.

But she *was* tired, and that made it all the easier for her to close her eyes and merely float off on that kiss.

She raised a hand to Ian's sculpted jaw, savoring, too, the texture of his skin as he deepened that kiss, as his arm went around her, pulling her closer—much the way he had during that last dance at the church. Only this was even better.

Jenna tipped her chin slightly more, taking another step in deepening that kiss, moving her hand to the back of his head, into the coarseness of his hair.

His mouth opened wider over hers, and Jenna followed his lead, working to keep from moaning with pleasure at the massage he was doing between her shoulder blades, shedding even more of the shouldn'ts that tried to creep into her mind and instead relinquishing everything to that kiss, which was so sweet, so sensual, so all consuming that she devoted herself to it, to Ian.

Their mouths opened even wider to form the passageway for tongues to meet, to circle and to frolic.

Ian stopped fingering her hair and cradled her head in his hand, bracing her against the kiss that was growing more intense, more powerful, more potent.

Oh, but it was such a great kiss!

It was as if she were discovering kissing all over again. The way she had as a girl, when kissing had been new. Only this was so much better. Ian was so much better.

And the same way it had felt only natural to lay her cheek to his chest when they'd danced, this also seemed right, perfect, as if they were both where they were meant to be, doing what they were meant to do. There was just something about this man that seemed to fit....

She wanted it to go on forever, just the way they were—kissing, tongues jousting and playing, feeling his hair between her fingers, his palm cupping her head, his other hand at her back, her breasts against his chest, just kissing and kissing and kissing....

And then maybe there could be more than kissing?

Ohh...

She must be too tired, a little voice somewhere in her brain warned her.

Maybe there could be more than kissing?

Where had that come from?

Okay, she knew where it was coming from—from that sudden awareness of her breasts against his chest, from that kiss heating up and lighting sparks inside her.

But more than kissing?

Yes, sure, her body was crying out in favor of it.

But she knew she was exhausted. And quite possibly not thinking straight. And she worried she'd lost her inhibitions the same way she hadn't had qualms about being nosy earlier, about prying into Ian's private business. If it went beyond kissing, it might be a mistake....

The kissing was so, so great, though....

She didn't want it to end.

And then Ian's hand moved from her back to her side and as much as she just wanted him to keep going, to find his way under the crocheted hem of her sweater, to breasts that felt swollen inside of her bra, to nipples that had hardened into pebbles, she knew she shouldn't—couldn't—let this go any further.

Her hand drifted out of his hair, and she moved it to his chest, pressing her palm there with just enough firmness to relay the message.

Still, he went on kissing her, exploring her mouth, teasing her tongue. He held her hand to his chest, gently coaxing her to yield to him.

But just to make sure he was getting the message, Jenna cooled the kiss, too, sending her tongue on a retreat from the circle dance it had been doing with his.

Ian gave in, slowly retracing the steps that had gotten them there until—to Jenna's sorrow—the kiss ended.

"Yeah," he said with a raspier voice, obviously agreeing to stop, even if he didn't want to any more than she did.

Then, with a resigned sigh, he got up from the couch and held out a hand for her to join him.

Without thinking about it, Jenna clasped his hand and stood up, letting him lead her to the front door.

There was no reason for him to hold her hand the whole way, but he did. And she certainly didn't balk. But once they got to the entry, he squeezed his fingers tightly around hers then let go, grabbing his jacket from the coatrack.

He put on his coat and reached for the doorknob. Then he looked at her and smiled just before he clasped the back of her neck and brought her to him so he could kiss her again—a long, sexy kiss that made her knees weak.

"I guess we better try not to have such a good time together, huh?" he joked as he freed her.

"We'll have to put a concerted effort into it tomorrow night," Jenna confirmed, making him grin.

"Yeah, we'll have to," he said. "I'll see what I can do about that."

Then they exchanged good-nights, and Ian let himself out.

With her lips still warm from that parting kiss, Jenna stared after him.

Working hard to recall why it was that she was supposed to deny herself something that she wanted so much.

Chapter Eight

"I don't know why you've been watching the door all night, but you just missed someone coming in. Someone who looks just like you and I'm wondering if you've been expecting him…."

"You noticed the door-watching, huh?" Ian said in response to Jenna's comment. He had been watching the entrance to the new section of Adz—a special room behind the game area that could be reserved for private parties like tonight's rehearsal dinner. But he'd gone to get Jenna one of the molten chocolate lava cakes for dessert, and during that time, his back had been to the doorway.

Standing near the fireplace, Jenna merely pointed her chin in the direction of the door to urge him to take a look now.

Despite that, it still wasn't easy for him to pull his eyes away from her. Her hair was falling free and silky around her face. She was wearing a black lace turtleneck top that played peekaboo around a solid black camisole and a pair of black slacks that made his hands itch to reach out and pat her rump.

But he knew that at that particular moment, he had to pull his attention away from Jenna and deal with the arrival of his brother.

"Yeah, Hutch is coming to the wedding." He told Jenna the news he'd known for most of the day. The news that he'd kept to himself because he'd realized that it was going to provoke a number of questions that he didn't want to answer until he could tell Jenna—of all people—the whole story.

"This is big, isn't it?" she asked, those beautiful greenish-brown eyes of hers round with the curiosity he'd anticipated.

"Big enough, I guess," Ian answered. He handed her the lava cake and leaned in closer to her ear to whisper, "Save me a couple of bites of this, I'll be back." Then he left Jenna with the luscious dessert and turned to face the music. And the brother he hadn't seen in nearly six years.

The brother who was carrying a small child when Ian met them halfway.

"Hutch," he greeted simply.

"Ian," Hutch said in the same tone.

When Chase and Shannon had contacted Ian, his long-lost brother and sister had asked how to reach Hutch. Ian had given them the last email address he had for his twin but had been clear about the fact that he and Hutch were on the outs.

Since then, Ian was aware that Shannon and Chase

had contacted Hutch—that they'd spoken to Hutch on the phone and emailed him, that Chase and Shannon had gone to meet him in Denver in February and that Shannon had invited him to her wedding.

They'd been open with Ian about everything to do with Hutch, including the invitation and the fact that Hutch wasn't sure if he was going to be able to make it to the wedding. When Hutch had decided at the last minute on Friday that he could, he'd emailed Ian directly.

There had been little to the email except to say that he wouldn't attend the wedding if it would cause any problems for Ian.

But Ian had moved past the hard feelings that had caused the rift in the first place and decided that this coming together of siblings was a good time to bury the hatchet with Hutch, too. So Ian had emailed a reply to Hutch that he had no problem with seeing his twin at Shannon's wedding.

So it was no surprise to Ian that Hutch was there.

It was, however, the first time Ian had laid eyes on Hutch's child. The child Ian had only heard through the grapevine that his brother had had with the woman Ian had once been engaged to.

"It's good to see you," Hutch finally said.

"You, too," Ian responded. "And this would be…" He glanced at the small boy slung on his brother's hip.

"Ash. Asher. Your nephew. Can you say hi, Ash?" Hutch asked his son. "This is your Uncle Ian."

The small child merely frowned at Ian and said nothing.

"He's not quite two and a half," Hutch explained. "It takes him a little while to warm up."

"Hi, Asher. Nice to meet you," Ian said to the child, ignoring his standoffishness.

Asher's only response was to put the two middle fingers of one hand in his mouth.

Ian glanced back at Hutch. It was like looking at his own reflection in a mirror—somehow even their haircuts were similar. "I heard about Iris—only not until a month after her accident when I ran into her cousin. I'm sorry."

"Thanks. I kept the memorial private. There wasn't even an obituary. I let her brother Dwayne know and he went from there notifying her family, but since we hadn't talked to you or the old man in so long before that, I just decided—"

"Yeah," Ian said, putting himself in his brother's shoes, knowing how awkward the situation was. This woman had caused a serious rift in their family; it didn't seem likely that her death would be the catalyst for mending fences. "You could have, though," he assured Hutch.

"Yeah," Hutch said, as if he knew that. "But I was kind of a mess and I did more withdrawing than reaching out to anybody. I didn't really want to reach out to anybody…."

Ian nodded his understanding.

"Everything I hear about Dad says he's doing well, though," Hutch said then. "I'm sure he's in his glory over finally getting his own football team."

"He is. But he'll still be glad to see you," Ian said.

"That's next on the list. Since Iris died I patched things up with Dwayne—he's been beating himself up for losing the last years he could have had with Iris, and he wanted to get to know his nephew. It got me to thinking about all the time you and I have lost, all the time I've lost with the old man. Then there was Chase and Shannon coming out of the woodwork—"

"Yeah, how was that for a shock? We had a brother and sisters all along?"

"That took some sinking in," Hutch said. "But it made me think even more about family, about reconnecting, about how Ash should know he's a part of something bigger…. Anyway, I've been trying to find the right time. I wasn't sure this was it, but then the weekend cleared unexpectedly and it seemed like a sign. So…."

"I'm glad you came," Ian said, meaning it. He hadn't been sure if some residual resentment might rise to the surface when he saw his brother again, but he was glad to find that there wasn't any. So he said what was going through his mind. "What happened is in the past. I know I did my share of being out of line—there was no real reason you and Iris couldn't get together, she and I were history at that point, and I don't have any hard feelings. If you don't—"

"I don't," Hutch said.

"Then let's just put it behind us."

Hutch held out his hand. "And move on."

Ian accepted his twin's outstretched hand and shook it.

Seeing that, Asher held out his hand to Ian, too, and—with a laugh—Ian shook that one as well.

"A kid?" he said then to Hutch on a much less stilted note.

"I know, weird, isn't it? I'm a dad."

"And he looks just like us," Ian marveled.

"*Just* like us," Hutch confirmed.

For a moment, Ian stared at the child, thinking that that was what he wanted when he was ready to have kids of his own—that kind of obvious, irrefutable bond….

"Where are you staying?" Ian asked.

"Shannon offered me Dag's house while they go on their honeymoon. And speaking of sisters—how's Lacey?"

Their younger sister had been caught in the middle of the Kincaid family feud and fearing that she might make things worse if she kept a foot in both camps, she'd conceded to their father. She hadn't had contact with Hutch in all this time, either.

"Lacey is terrific," Ian said. "She's hated this whole mess, though. She'll love it if it all ends."

"If?"

"When. Dad wants it over, too. If you extend an olive branch, he'll take it."

Hutch nodded. "I wouldn't want Ash to grow up not knowing the only grandfather he has."

"If you can stay in Northbridge after the wedding, he'll be here next week—I can bring the two of you together…."

"As long as the old man is willing, that would be good," Hutch agreed.

"Great! Then come on, I'll buy you a drink and there's someone I want you to meet…."

Jenna was waiting.

After watching Ian come face-to-face with his estranged brother at the rehearsal dinner, Ian had brought Hutch to her to introduce them.

"I'll fill you in on everything later…." Ian had whispered in her ear.

But later hadn't come during the remainder of the evening at Adz. It also hadn't come on the drive back to the Mackey and McKendrick compound where a babysitter was watching the children tonight.

After finding that Abby was asleep, Jenna agreed to Meg's suggestion that Abby spend the night with her since Jenna would be back early the next morning to get ready for the wedding anyway. Which left Jenna free to accept Ian's invitation to have a glass of wine in the small studio apartment above Meg's garage where he was staying. Hopefully now she'd get to hear what Ian had to say about his twin.

She was sitting on a bar stool at the island counter that separated the kitchen from the living room, waiting. He was on the other side of the counter opening the wine but still not saying anything of consequence.

Not that watching him was an unpleasant distraction. He was dressed in charcoal-gray slacks and a dove-gray dress shirt with the sleeves rolled to his elbows. Until his brother had walked in to provide a mirror image of him tonight, Jenna had considered him the best looking man in the room. And even after meeting his brother, looking back and forth between them, marveling at just how much they did look alike, Jenna had still decided that she preferred Ian's more tailored look to the casual air that Hutch had about him. So getting a private show of him opening and pouring the wine now was hardly a trial.

But still she was dying to know what had happened

between the brothers—both to cause the rift and now to mend it—and she was tired of waiting.

"Okay, I'm on pins and needles!" she said when Ian slid a glass of red wine across the bar to her, and he bent forward to lean his forearms on the counter with his own glass cupped between his hands. "You said you'd fill me in—so fill me in! You knew your brother was coming tonight?"

"I did," he admitted. He explained how he'd known, how he'd even given his approval to the idea.

"And were you *really* okay with him coming, or did you just say so because it wasn't your place to keep him away from Shannon's wedding?"

"I was really okay with it," he said, and it sounded like the truth. "I've had time to think about what it would be like to see him again since I first found out Shannon and Chase had gotten hold of him. I just realized that what had aggravated me six years ago didn't aggravate me anymore. And by this morning, I thought that I was ready to forget about everything and get past it."

"And do I get to know what happened between you that caused the rift?" Jenna asked hopefully, sipping her wine.

"Her name was Iris Stinson—"

"There's an Iris and a Chelsea?" Jenna heard herself blurt out before she'd even thought about it.

Ian squinted his pale blue eyes at her. "How do you know about Chelsea?"

Too late to lie. "I overheard your father talking to you about her that day you brought him to the farm."

"Ah," Ian said. But he wasn't flustered in any way by the fact that Jenna knew about the other woman. And he certainly didn't seem to feel any kind of guilt or embarrassment, nor did he give any indication that he'd been caught at something.

Instead he said, "Well, yeah, I do know a Chelsea, and there was an Iris. And there *are* some similarities in things with the two of them, namely what my father hopes—and hoped—to accomplish through them. Chelsea's father owns Tanner Brewery and getting Tanner Brewery as a sponsor for the Monarchs would be a coup. My father would love it if Chelsea fell madly in love with me and Tanner Brewery became a permanent sponsor through marriage. Chelsea is a model and she works mainly in Europe. *Her* father would like it if she didn't. He wants her to be closer to home. He wants me to sell her on becoming the face of Tanner Brewery as the Monarchs' sponsor and he's hinted that he also wouldn't mind seeing her settle down, married, having a few grandchildren. I'm working on Chelsea doing advertisements—"

"In exchange for your playlist?"

Ian laughed. "Oh, you really *were* listening that day. Chelsea likes obscure jazz and so do I. It's common ground, a common interest that I'm using to cultivate a business relationship—we'd be playing golf if she golfed. But cultivating a business relationship through a common interest is *all* that's between Chelsea and I. As we speak she's juggling three men on two different continents—that's part of why her father would like to see her settle down. But *I* am *not* one of the three men, and I have no desire to be number four."

Jenna studied him, looking for signs that he was lying or downplaying the whole Chelsea issue.

But she believed him.

Then, in a more serious vein, he said, "Iris, on the other hand, was something else entirely."

Iris, on the other hand, had her even more curious.

"What was your father hoping to accomplish through this Iris person?" Jenna asked.

"Iris was the younger sister of Dwayne Stinson, owner of the South Dakota Stingers."

"Another football team," Jenna said, thinking she'd heard the name before and putting two and two together when it came to the Kincaids and their focus on that particular sport.

"Another NFL football team, right. The one that recruited Hutch to play out of college. Even before Hutch joined the team, the Stingers had had some respectable seasons, but they also had some financial struggles. My father knew that and was hoping to parlay Hutch's connection with the team into his own partnership with Dwayne Stinson. My father wanted to be co-owner of the Stingers."

"He's been single-minded about achieving that goal, your father..."

"He has. From when he was still playing himself, he wanted to own an NFL football team. And he was looking to do that any way he could."

"And your brother opened that door for him."

"My father opens his own doors—sometimes he kicks them in—but one way or another, if he wants a door opened, it gets opened. But with Hutch on a team that had a weakness Morgan Kincaid could use to his advantage? Yeah, to Dad that looked like a door opening."

"And you went through the open door and found Iris?"

"Pretty much. Dwayne was a lot older than Iris and raised her after their parents died, so he was more like a father to her. They were close, Hutch fast became the Stingers' star player, my father was inching his way into team ownership, and I was family—*and* I was on the business end of things—so there started to be a lot of occasions when Iris and I were at the same functions."

"And you got together," Jenna guessed.

"We did. In fact, we were engaged."

Jenna felt her eyebrows arch as she took a sip of her wine.

"You were engaged but you didn't get married?" she asked after her sip.

"Engaged but never married—right. That's the closest I've ever come."

"But you didn't get there…." she said to prompt more of the story.

"Iris had some trouble deciding what she wanted to do," Ian continued. "She'd been in and out of half a dozen different colleges and triple that many majors, all without graduating. Jobs went the same way—she just couldn't seem to settle on anything. And then she announced that she wanted to be a part of the business end of football."

"And she'd cried wolf so often—"

"Right—neither Dwayne nor I took her seriously. Dwayne said she was flighty, that wanting to work for the Stingers was just another one of her whims. There was no way he was giving her anything to do with his team. So she came to me."

That sounded ominous, and the fact that Ian threw back what remained of his wine and rounded the counter to sit on the bar stool facing Jenna only added to the weight of his words.

"Iris wanted me to go to her brother on her behalf," he said, his tone a sort of sigh. "She wanted me to point out to him that she'd been immersed in everything to do with football her whole life, that it was the normal progression of things, that that was what she had the most aptitude for, that that's where her real interests lay—stuff that made a certain amount of sense."

"But there was her track record."

"Exactly. Which was what Dwayne said when I had a drink with him and brought it up. And not only was he one hundred percent against the very idea of giving Iris any shot with the Stingers since the team was already in some financial jeopardy, he advised me to just sit back and wait until this fad blew over, too." Ian shrugged. "And that's the position I took."

And his tone was even more ominous than it had been before.

"It didn't do a lot for your relationship," Jenna surmised.

"Tanked it. Iris got madder and madder at my not taking her seriously. She thought I was siding with her brother instead of her when I should be going to bat for her with Dwayne and convincing him that he should give her a chance—which I couldn't do because he was adamant. She accused me of being as bad as her brother, of not seeing who she was or giving her credit for anything. Ultimately, she broke the engagement."

"I'm sorry," Jenna said.

Ian shrugged his broad shoulders. "It was a blow," he admitted. "It was also the first time I'd been dumped," he added with some chagrin. "So there had to be some wound-licking, but I got over it."

"Did that do damage with the other connections—your father trying to buy into her brother's team or your brother playing for it?"

"Actually, no, that didn't do any harm. That was—" he seemed to be calculating in his head before he said "—a little over six and a half years ago. The harm came about seven months later. The dust had settled over the end of the engagement, I'd moved on and was actually dating someone else—my rebound, I suppose, because nothing came of it. But that was when Hutch's contract with the Stingers was up…."

Jenna finished her wine, and declined a second glass when Ian offered it, because she still needed to drive home.

Then to urge him to go on, she said, "So your brother's contract was up…."

"Right. And Iris went to him and talked him into becoming a free agent, represented by her."

"Really?" Jenna said, thinking that she had to admire the other woman's determination to prove herself.

"Yep. Dad had negotiated Hutch's previous contract, and Hutch knew that the old man had had his own buying-into-the-Stingers interests at heart when he'd done it. Hutch said he liked Iris's enthusiasm, her drive, and he decided to let her see what she could do for him."

"The plot thickens," Jenna said. "Had anything been going on between them before?"

"Like when she was engaged to me? Nah. I mean, they

knew each other, of course. But Hutch dated around—he did exactly what the old man disapproved of and reaped the benefits of sports fame with a progression of football groupies. So beyond knowing each other, no, he and Iris weren't involved. Even when she talked him into letting her represent him, it was a purely business arrangement." Another raise of just one brow. "Until it wasn't. Which was about the time all hell broke loose."

"What happened?"

"Iris actually turned out to be a good agent—she got Hutch a much better contract with another team. A team the Stingers ended up losing to every time they met them during the three years Hutch played for them. Dwayne was furious with Hutch for leaving and with Iris for brokering the deal. He took it out on Dad and said he'd see the Stingers go into bankruptcy rather than take a nickel of Dad's money and let him in on a team his son had left hanging out to dry. And then Dad turned that around on me—"

"How did that happen?" Jenna asked, confused.

"The old man was in a rage—he'd been so close to finally getting what he wanted and then the rug was pulled out from under him. He started in on me about how none of it would have ever happened if I'd just married Iris—"

"No? Seriously?" Jenna said in disbelief.

"Seriously. We had a blowout. By then Hutch and Iris had hooked up, and even though I didn't have any feelings left for her, I didn't want to see her with my *brother* of all people. It just seemed so damn disloyal for him to get involved with her. And for me to be taking the brunt of Dad's wrath because of what he was doing only made it worse. Hutch and I fought, and…" Yet another shrug. "There you have it. I left the Kincaid Corporation for a while—until the old man came to me, apologized, said he was out of line and being ridiculous to blame me—"

"Which he was."

Ian conceded that with a tilt of his head before he went on with what he was saying, "Anyway, the old man asked me to come back to work on the Monarchs, and we've been okay since then. But tonight was the first time Hutch and I have been in the same room since."

There was one final piece that was missing and Jenna wasn't sure how touchy a subject it might be, but she just couldn't leave it alone. So with some care, she said, "I heard something tonight about Iris being killed?"

"About a year ago. In a skiing accident."

"And neither you nor your father went to Hutch even then?"

"We didn't even know about it until a month later. By then… Well, we'd only found out through the grapevine that Iris and Hutch had gotten married, that they'd had a baby. We'd accepted the fact that he didn't want us around for any of that. Since he didn't so much as have someone else call to say Iris had died, we figured he must not have wanted us in on that either. You know how these things—family fights—are. Holes get dug deeper and deeper, and they're pretty tough to get out of."

"But today…"

"I just thought that enough was enough. Dad and I both hated not being around for the arrival of Hutch's first child. Dad's first grandson. My first nephew. Then not being there for Hutch when his wife died? It seemed wrong. It felt wrong. But… You know, when you haven't spoken for years, when he hasn't seemed to want you around…"

Ian shook his head, and Jenna thought that whether or not he realized that he had any regrets, he did—he regretted what had gone on within his family.

"But like I said, enough was enough, and since Hutch was willing, I wasn't going to let this thing go on any longer than it has. Now I'll get him together with the old man—Dad will be glad to have it over with, too—and that'll put an end to it."

Jenna laughed. "That's it? A little spackle, some paint—good as new?"

"Sure. Why not?" he asked.

"No talking about what went on, no resolving issues, no discussion about what was done that shouldn't have been done and how to avoid it happening again?"

"No!" he said, as if he hated the thought. "What would any of that change? We'll go with the spackle and paint and be good as new."

Jenna nodded. "Well, I suppose that's worked for generations of cavemen before you, so it'll probably work for you now."

"Cavemen?" he repeated with a laugh of his own.

"You can clean yourselves up and dress in well-cut pants and shirts that make women *think* you've evolved, but underneath it all, you're still cavemen," she observed more out of admiration for how Ian in particular cleaned up than in condemnation for his overly simplistic goal of solving a years' long family rift.

Ian merely smiled a wicked smile. "So you've been thinking about what's underneath the shirt and pants?"

Jenna laughed again. "*That's* what you took from what I said? You are a caveman." But yes, she did frequently wonder what his body looked like. And then reprimanded herself for it.

Ian perched on the very edge of his bar stool until his legs straddled hers and took hold of her seat on either side, pulling it near enough for them to be almost nose to nose.

"And here you are, in my cave…." he pointed out.

With her wine finished and her curiosity satisfied, she said, "Mmm… But I should probably get going. Tomorrow's a big day, and I want to be over here again early, when Abby wakes up."

And yet leaving couldn't be easily accomplished now that Ian had boxed her in.

Not that she was making any move in that direction. She wasn't. She was sitting exactly as she had been, answering his steady gaze with an intensity of her own.

Oh, those blue eyes!

And that handsome face. And the clean, woodsy scent of his cologne. And that dimple he had in the very center of his chin…

Somehow, her index finger had found its way to that chin, to trace the rise, the dip, the second rise….

He leaned farther forward and kissed her then, and her hand slid to the side of his face—clean shaven but still rougher than her own skin—as she kissed him in return.

Even as she did, she drew a deep breath and told herself she shouldn't be kissing him. Again. But it seemed like she spent every minute she *wasn't* kissing him, thinking about kissing him, recalling each kiss they'd shared, wanting to kiss him again. So when it actually happened? She couldn't make herself *not* kiss him.

She couldn't even make herself remember why she shouldn't.

Instead, her eyes drifted closed, and in that instant, kissing him was all there was. His mouth on hers. His lips parting over hers. Hers parting, too. Her tongue meeting his, welcoming it.

He stroked her hair, cradling her head to deepen the kiss. His other arm went around her and pulled her to the edge of her seat until her knees were a mere fraction of an inch from the juncture of his legs.

She tried not to think about that. But with their kiss intensifying, with his hand rubbing her back and making her think about what she wanted him to do to other parts of her, it was impossible not to think about *his* body being so close.

Her own breasts seemed to be straining within the confines of her binding camisole. Her nipples were nudging against the soft fabric, tempting her with cravings all their own. Cravings to feel his touch. To feel the warmth of his hands on them.

What was she doing? she asked herself, knowing full well that she shouldn't be doing this. That she shouldn't be doing anything with him.

So go home, Jen, she silently commanded.

But his mouth opened wider over hers. He held her head and leaned into that kiss. His tongue grew wilder and more abandoned. And that hand at her back wasn't at her back any longer—it was on the side of her rib cage, its heel riding the outermost swell of her breast….

And she wanted—she *needed*—to know what it

would be like to have his hand curve around her. She couldn't deny it. She couldn't deny herself.

Another deep breath gave Ian the invitation he needed. He answered it by giving her what she wanted so desperately at that moment—his hand slowly moved to cup her breast.

Yes, there was a camisole and lace top between his fingers and her naked flesh but it still felt so good that Jenna couldn't keep from expanding within his grasp, from pressing her nipple all the more into his palm.

His fingers closed around her, cocooning her, massaging, rubbing, pressing into her with the perfect pressure, the perfect firmness, the perfect mixture of playfulness, pleasure and reverence.

The perfect everything except for the clothes that acted as a barricade to keep her from actually feeling the texture, the heat, the intimacy of his bare skin encasing hers.

Still kissing her, tongues still playing and parrying, he eased her off the bar stool to stand in the lee of his legs. Then, as if he knew what she wanted most, his hand finally found its way to the lacy edge of her shirt and slipped underneath.

Big and warm, slightly callused—that hand coursed up her naked side and rediscovered her breast, grasping it the way she'd longed for him to, skin to skin. Her nipple found its true, unabashed nesting place in his bare palm as his fingers pressed into her flesh.

Jenna's arms went around him, and she tugged his shirttails from his waistband, driven to feel what she'd only imagined was beneath his clothes. To feel the broad shoulders only hinted at by well-cut clothing. To find out for herself if his back, his chest, were as hard and honed and muscular as they seemed to be.

Satin over steel—he was sleek and smooth and solid as rock.

And he felt so good.

Almost as good as it felt to have him doing what he was doing to her breast, teasing, tugging her nipple, flattening his palm to the very crest and driving her just a little insane.

Then he pulled her in closer still. Close enough for her to feel his own body's response.

And she wanted to know more of that, too. More of him.

They could take it another step. *She* could take it another step, and she had no doubt where Ian would go from there. Maybe whisk her off to that bed that was just across the room. Or lift her up onto the counter and…

And what?

She knew what.

And she wanted it to happen.

But something inside of her hesitated. For a mere instant.

Yet it was enough for reason to creep in. For something to remind her that she needed to get her life on track. That she needed to get settled. To focus. To get accustomed to being a mother to Abby. To make a home for them both.

That she needed *not* to live in the moment, especially not now that she'd taken on the responsibility of a child. Especially not just when she was starting off on a new path for herself.

Especially when none of what she wanted at that

instant, none of what her entire body was crying out for, seemed to be in line with those new responsibilities or that new path.

The quiet sigh that escaped her then wasn't only in response to the incredible things Ian was doing to first one breast and then the other. It was because she knew she had to stop him before this went on any longer. Before she *couldn't* stop him, couldn't refuse herself what she wanted more and more with every passing second.

And no, it didn't help that when she went to push herself even slightly away from him, her hand was still under his shirt and she was pressing against an amazing pectoral.

But she pushed anyway.

And then forced herself to take her hand out from under his shirt.

There was one, final, deep caress of her breast.

One final duet with her tongue.

One final, simple, open kiss.

And then Ian stopped.

Jenna opened her eyes just in time to watch him tip his head far back, to watch his jaw tighten, his Adam's apple bob with a swallow, to watch Ian working to gain some control.

Then he slowly brought his handsome face level with hers again, took a breath, exhaled it and said, "We were supposed to avoid having such a good time together tonight, weren't we?"

His raspy, passion-ragged voice was so sexy she nearly wilted, and it didn't help her resolve one bit.

"We were," was the best she could manage as she fought for control of her own.

"I'm not sure what happens to me when I'm with you," he confided. "I talk more than I ever have—with anybody. I kind of slip out of time and space and forget…well…everything else."

She understood. The same thing happened to her. At least until some common sense injected itself.

"We do seem to have a knack for getting carried away," she agreed.

"Yes, we do," he said with a smile that made her think he wasn't altogether sorry for that.

Then he took his arms from around her, held them out as if in surrender and gave her the opening she knew she should take to put some distance between them.

She couldn't quite make herself take it immediately, but after arguing with herself a moment more, she turned and moved toward the apartment door, grabbing her coat from the sofa along the way.

Ian took the long wool dress coat from her before she realized what he was doing and held it for her to slip on.

"I hate that you're driving home alone. I could take you, then pick you up in the morning and bring you back," he offered as she pivoted around to face him while she buttoned her coat.

"It's a five-minute drive that I make a dozen times a week," she said with a smile, imagining him taking her home right now and knowing that once they got there, there wouldn't be much of a chance of him leaving again.

"I'll see you tomorrow then, I guess," he said, taking both of her upper arms in his big, strong hands, and rubbing them up and down.

"Bright and early," Jenna confirmed. "And tomorrow night for the wedding."

Something about that made him smile again—a broad, pleased grin, as if the thought of the wedding the following evening made her leaving now easier to accept.

But he merely nodded, his eyes on her, studying her once more.

Then he pulled her closer, leaning forward himself and giving her a kiss so sweet, so deep, that it roused everything in her all over again before he cut it short and let go of her.

This time Jenna didn't hesitate to take the opening, because she knew that if she didn't she wasn't going anywhere tonight.

So after repeating that she'd see him the next day, she went out into the cold March night, descended the steps that ran alongside the garage wall and made a beeline for her car parked beside the compound's main house.

Not until she was safely behind the wheel did she glance up those same stairs to see if she'd been right in thinking that Ian had followed her out and was still watching her.

He had. And he was still standing there, bathed in the glow of porch lights, tall and handsome and making her ache to go back up there to him.

But Jenna stomped on that inclination and gave herself a laundry list of reasons why she needed to start her engine and drive away.

Which she ultimately did.

And yet, willpower or no willpower, it wasn't that laundry list of reasons that went home with her, that went to bed with her, that kept her awake much, much longer than she should have been.

It was thoughts of Ian that did that.

It was reliving his every kiss. His every touch. Wanting to be with him so much she could hardly bear it.

And worrying at the same time how she was going to spend five minutes with him the next night and not finish what they'd started…

Chapter Nine

The wedding of Ian's newfound sister Shannon Duffy to Dag McKendrick was held Sunday evening at the small chapel that served all denominations of Northbridge's religious needs.

Shannon's colors were black and bright yellow—like the sunflowers that stood out among the wildflowers that decorated both the church and the bouquets.

Shannon's gown was a simple, form-fitting white satin held up by spaghetti straps. It fell to the tops of her sequined shoes and sported a long train in back that draped from the top of the dress to give a cape effect.

She wore her hair in a burst of curls caught at her crown. Her elbow-length veil was attached by a circle of pearls around the updo, and there was no question that she made a beautiful bride.

Her matron of honor was her best friend Dani Bond, who had come from Beverly Hills with her husband.

Hadley, Meg and Jenna were her bridesmaids. Chase gave her away, then joined Logan—the best man—Ian and another of Logan and Dag's brothers as groomsmen.

The ceremony was short, sweet and touching, and Jenna tried not to cry at the beauty of it and at the sadness of recalling taking those same vows and having them now broken.

But she worked at keeping the sadness at bay—in no small part by repeatedly glancing across the altar at Ian, whose very presence, for no reason she understood, seemed to bolster her, calm her and lighten her sad feelings. And despite those sad feelings, she hoped Shannon and Dag would have better luck than she had had.

After the ceremony, the reception was held in the church basement where there was a buffet full of food, music for dancing and a four-tiered cake adorned in remarkably realistic-looking fondant replicas of the real wildflowers.

It was at the reception where Abby seemed to adopt Ian as her own personal date. While she had made her fondness for him clear before, tonight she refused to be let out of his arms.

Jenna was embarrassed that the infant threw a fit every time she or anyone else tried to take Abby. She also screamed and cried and put Ian in a stranglehold the minute he attempted to set her down.

"I hope you have this kind of effect on grown women," Hadley, Chase's wife of only a few months, teased him when she and Chase joined Ian and Jenna at their table.

"If he did," Chase goaded with a grin, "they'd be lined up outside the door."

"I should be so lucky," Ian joked.

But he ended up carrying Abby through the buffet line while Jenna filled his plate and hers, hers with enough food for her and Abby.

While they ate, he held Abby on his lap, and Jenna fed her.

And when it came to dancing, the infant wouldn't relinquish Ian to Jenna then, either. The best the tiny child allowed was for the three of them to dance together with Abby perched on one of Ian's hips—her arm wrapped possessively around his neck—while his free arm went around Jenna. Jenna was left to place one hand on his chest and her other arm around man and child.

"Apparently I am still just the spare tire," Jenna observed as the three of them danced that way for the third time. "You and I were supposed to keep each other from that fate, but now it seems I'm hanging on to the tails of you and Abby. I think she has a full-blown crush on you."

"It's the tux," Ian said, as if he were giving away a secret.

Jenna laughed, but thought he might be right. He *did* look amazing in the black tuxedo with the crisp white shirt and dark tie. And the minute Abby had set eyes on him looking so dashing and handsome, the baby had latched on to him.

"Maybe she figures she's all dressed up in her frilly dress and patent-leather shoes, so she needs an escort," Jenna suggested.

"Never mind that you look pretty good yourself," Ian complimented her, with admiration in his tone.

Jenna was wearing the same style of dress that the rest of the female members of the wedding party were wearing—simple knee-length shifts that were as curve hugging as Shannon's wedding dress was, only fashioned of black lace over bright yellow strapless sheaths, sleeveless, with boat necks.

"Well, she is letting me share you," Jenna commented as they mostly swayed to the music. "I suppose I should be grateful for that."

And in truth, the entire evening had been kind of nice. Nice that the three of them had enjoyed it together. Nice that Abby liked Ian so much. Nice that Ian was so receptive to the fifteen-month-old's adoration when another sort of person might have been annoyed by it.

"But it looks like someone is wearing out," Jenna whispered when Abby put her weary little head on Ian's shoulder.

It was after nine o'clock by then, long past Abby's bedtime.

Ian glanced down at the infant and then kissed her forehead in a way that made it seem as if it wasn't something he'd thought about ahead of time.

But after that, his focus was all on Jenna. "Something struck me as we were standing at the altar during the ceremony," he said, making Jenna wonder if he'd caught her sneaking a peek at him once too often.

If he had, that wasn't what he was referring to, though, because he said, "You and Shannon can't have known each other for long. Chase didn't locate her until last fall, and Christmas was when she came to Northbridge for the first time...."

"We did just meet after the first of the year. But we had a lot in common—loss, actually—and we became friends while commiserating with each other. We sort of formed an instant kinship."

Ian nodded his understanding and then returned to his earlier compliment with a somewhat more breathy tone, "Well, you *do* make a beautiful bridesmaid...." he said, pulling her in as close as possible with Abby between them.

That was nice, too, and Jenna didn't shrink away from him. Actually, she used placing a kiss of her own on Abby's chubby cheek as an excuse to then tuck her head under Ian's chin.

But all too soon, that song ended, a fast one began and Jenna had to step out of his arms.

Abby was half asleep on Ian's shoulder, and with a nod at her, he said, "Want to swipe a couple of pieces of cake to take home? We can get Abby to bed and then have them."

Several guests had already left, they wouldn't be the first to depart. And taking Abby home to bed would finally give Ian a break from her.

Or at least, that was what Jenna told herself rather than acknowledge that the idea of going back to the farm, of having Ian to herself, had more appeal than it should have had.

"You don't mind leaving early?" she asked him.

"Nah. I can get out of this coat and tie to really enjoy the cake," he said with a smile that insinuated something more.

That was as much convincing as Jenna needed to set the wheels of saying good-night into motion.

Abby was sound asleep by the time she, Jenna and Ian reached the farm. Ian carried in the car seat—baby and all—and brought it upstairs for Jenna.

While Jenna took the sleeping Abby out of her party dress, changed her diaper, got her into her pajamas and tucked into her crib, Ian went back downstairs. When Jenna got there, he was waiting for her with their two pieces of wedding cake on the coffee table, his tux jacket and tie gone and the collar button of his shirt opened. And he was in the center of the sofa, angled in anticipation of Jenna joining him there.

While she'd been upstairs, Jenna had cast off her shoes and the panty hose that had been strangling her. Now she sat sideways on the sofa to face Ian and tucked her bare feet under her rump.

"Ah, cake," she said with a glutton's glee as she reached for the two paper plates on the coffee table and handed one to Ian.

"It's good, too," he assured her. He took a bite of the confection of raspberry-chocolate ganache layered between chocolate cake, all nestled within white buttercream frosting.

"Mmm," Jenna agreed, closing her eyes for a moment to truly get the full enjoyment out of her own bite.

Ian was grinning at her when she opened her eyes again. "You really like cake," he said with a laugh.

Jenna laughed, too. "You were right—it is good," she said to conceal just how much of a sweet tooth she had.

"So," he said while they ate, "you said you and Shannon became friends commiserating over the losses you'd both suffered. You both lost family members, but I know for Shannon there was also the long-term relationship she had with Wes Rumson—potentially the next Governor of Montana. Did your marriage end last year, too?" he asked, referring to Jenna's earlier explanation about what had led her and his new sister to become close friends so quickly.

"It was," she answered. "I was divorced last summer."

"After how many years?"

"If we had made it to December, it would have been ten years."

"You got married right out of high school?"

"The Christmas after. During my first year of college, Ted's last, just before Ted graduated with his bachelor's degree. Ted, that's his name. Ted Gunderson. We were high-school sweethearts—I tutored him in chemistry."

"A senior needed to be tutored by a freshman?"

Jenna shrugged and went on. "I was a freshman, but I was in advanced classes. His mother was determined that her son be a doctor, and everyone around here knew that was the track I'd put myself on, so she wanted us to study together. During the course of that, we started to like each other. He asked me to the winter dance, and we were together from then on."

"His mother was determined that he be a doctor? Does that mean that he *wasn't* determined?"

Another shrug, this one more wishy-washy. "Let's just say that he was—*is*—determined to please his mother. Early on, I thought that becoming a doctor was a dream we shared—Ted and I. But on his side, the dream was all his mother's."

"Did he become a doctor?"

"He's still trying…."

"Shouldn't he be one by now? I mean, you would be, wouldn't you? And he had a head start on you."

"I would have finished residency last year, so yes, I would be practicing now. And yes, he could have been.

Except that he's been in and out of five different residency programs and still hasn't decided what branch of medicine he can stand to actually do."

"Let me see if I have this straight," Ian said, taking her empty plate and setting it next to his on the coffee table. He then stretched an arm along the back of the sofa cushion and began to fiddle with her hair where it fell freely to her shoulders. "It was your dream, from when you were a kid, to be a doctor. You didn't end up a doctor, but the guy who needed you to tutor him actually did finish medical school but discovered he doesn't really like medicine?"

"I don't think he ever really liked it. Or wanted to be a doctor, to tell you the truth. But his dad died when he was only a baby, his mother raised him on her own—they're very close—and he doesn't want to disappoint her." Much the way Ian didn't want to disappoint his father, Jenna thought, but she didn't say that.

"And did this guy becoming a doctor derail you becoming a doctor?"

"I suppose so. Or at least I let myself be derailed. It was my choice to follow him to the college he got into. It wasn't really the college I wanted to go to, but it was the only one that accepted Ted, so when my time came, that was where I went, too. When he graduated and the only medical school he could get into was in Mexico, I could have said no to going with him—"

"But you'd married him at Christmas."

"Right. And that was the dilemma—did he give up medical school and crush his mother's dreams to stay in the states while I became a doctor instead of him? Or did I make the sacrifice?" she asked rhetorically.

"You made the sacrifice."

"Ted's idea was that we go to Mexico, and while he went to medical school, I could become a nurse. That way, I could still work in medicine, earn a living to support us and then, after he finished his training, he could open an office, and we could still work side by side—"

"With him as the doctor and you as the nurse?"

"Yes."

"You—the smarter of the two and the one who wanted to be a doctor from birth—should become a nurse to support him so he could become the doctor his mother wanted him to be? Was that what you *wanted* to do by then?" Ian asked.

"No, it wasn't," she said flatly. "I still wanted to be a doctor. But I thought that maybe once Ted was finished with school, I could apply to medical school after all."

"But that wasn't what happened, and instead it was you who sacrificed everything. You who gave up the dream you'd had all your life. No wonder you have regrets," Ian said, giving her earlobe a comforting sort of tug.

"Actually, my bigger regret was that, as the result of following Ted around, I neglected my own family." Her voice cracked.

"I imagine living in Mexico for four years made it tough to keep up with things here," Ian said quietly, apparently seeing that this was difficult for her.

"And Mexico was just the beginning. Even when we came back to the states for Ted to do his internship and residency, we lived all over the country. Ted would get into a program, decide he hated whatever branch of medicine he was training for, quit and apply somewhere else to try another specialty—"

"Which meant you had to change jobs, too."

"And find another place for us to live, get us moved and settled in. Then, because I was new to the job, I couldn't take time off to come home, so I rarely got back here. I barely made it to my sister's funeral, and I had to leave again so quick that even then I didn't see beyond the surface—I believed my folks were doing all right and able to take on Abby. When they said during every phone call that they were okay, that everything here was okay, I believed them. I didn't know what was *really* going on with them, with their health, with the farm, with anything because I wasn't *around!* I was following Ted's mother's dream…."

"And eventually you got fed up with it," Ian surmised.

"I finally gave Ted an ultimatum. We'd moved to Denver for a residency in cardiology, and after the first month, he was making his usual noises about how he didn't like it, about how it wasn't for him. I knew where that would go, and I told him that I'd had it. He said I wasn't being supportive, that I didn't understand. That he couldn't help it if he'd hated every kind of medicine he'd tried, that he had to keep trying until he found one he didn't hate, because he couldn't disappoint his mother by giving up." Jenna shook her head at the recollection.

"In other words, he wasn't going to be a cardiologist, either."

"No. I was at my wit's end. I told you that I'd decided that I liked nursing, so I wasn't hanging on to the idea of going to medical school myself anymore. But I wanted to settle in one place, I wanted to start a family—which I'd been pushing for for a few years, although Ted wouldn't even talk about it. I wanted to be able to reconnect with my folks, to help them with Abby, to be a part of Abby's life. I suggested we just come back here, that Ted go into family practice—which he could have done without any more training—and that maybe he would find his niche in the day-to-day of the job."

"And he wouldn't do it."

"In the first place, his mother had moved away from Northbridge by then—she's in Cincinnati now—and he said that wherever she was was where he was ending up. That Northbridge was out of the question. And as for going into family practice, he wouldn't even consider that either. He said he was going to try surgery next, that his mother would love to say her son was a surgeon, so he'd applied to a program in Iowa, and I should start sending my résumé to hospitals there…"

Ian dropped his head far forward, shook it in disbelief as he said, "No…."

"That's what I said," Jenna confirmed with a mirthless laugh. "I finally just said no. Basically, I told him to choose me, our marriage and actually starting a life together, or his mother and what she wanted even though it was obviously not what he wanted."

"And he chose wrong."

"He said that, regardless of what I might have sacrificed for him, his mother had raised him on her own and sacrificed more. He actually said that when it came down to his mother or me, his first loyalty was to his mother, and he was going to do whatever she wanted to make her happy. Whether I liked it or not. Whether I went along or not…." Jenna shrugged yet again and fought off the emotions that brought moisture to her eyes.

"And you decided you weren't going along anymore," Ian said the words she was having difficulty getting out.

Jenna nodded. "I filed for divorce, and as that was being finalized, and I was about to move back to Northbridge, my mom had her heart attack."

"Your sister died. Your mom died. Then you also found out about your dad's failing health and that the farm was in too much trouble to save, and there was Abby in need of a mom and—"

"And here I am."

"Whew!"

Somehow that eased some of her tension. Ian's comforting caress on the back of her neck helped, too.

"You must feel like you've been under some dark clouds for a while now," he said.

"A little bit," Jenna confirmed with a laugh to lighten the tone. "But nothing is ever simple, is it? We all make our choices, and we all have to live with them. And hopefully learn from them—the way you said you learned from your mistakes."

"You learned that you were happy being a nurse rather than a doctor…." Ian prodded, insinuating that he wanted to know what else she'd learned.

"For one. I also learned to stay away from any guy who isn't his own man and that I needed to make up my own mind about the path my life takes and not choose based on what's important to someone else."

"And not to always sacrifice what *you* want," he added, as if he thought she needed to be reminded of that.

"Well, I'm back in Northbridge where I want to be. I'm raising Abby, so I'm getting to start the family I wanted—even if it is a little unconventional." She smiled because she was about to goad him a little. "I'm not caving in to selling the farm to you. So all in all, I'd say that for now, I'm not sacrificing anything for anyone."

"Good for you!" he cheered. "Well, except that it would be *better* for you to sell the farm to me…."

Jenna laughed. "You can't let it go, can you?"

"Just thought I should point it out…." he said with such boyish charm that she couldn't help drinking him in. His handsomely sculpted features lit up with a smile as those pale blue eyes returned her gaze with a heat all their own.

Then, in a more serious tone, he added, "But I'm behind you all the way when it comes to doing what you want for a change."

And in the interest of doing what she wanted…

Ooo, that was a dangerous thought!

Dangerously tempting as she sat there looking into his eyes, feeling his hand on her nape, remembering so vividly how the night before had ended….

The memory of how she'd put such an abrupt halt to things, and how Ian had complied and left, had been haunting her all day.

Along with a torturous hankering for a better ending tonight.

She'd begun the day trying to figure out how to keep herself from succumbing to Ian when she was with him again.

Partway through the day, she'd found herself wondering why succumbing would be so bad.

She'd countered that by reminding herself why it would be.

But now…

Here they were again—only at her place rather than at the Mackey–McKendrick compound where there was less privacy.

Here she was again, barely inches away from Ian. And he certainly hadn't lost any appeal. He looked so good she couldn't take her eyes off him. He was sexier than any man she'd ever known. He smelled like heaven. He was rubbing her neck with a big strong hand. And everything he'd aroused in her the previous evening hovered just beneath the surface, wanting the chance to rise again, to be satisfied and soothed.

And what she *wanted* at that moment—what she truly wanted, *all* she wanted at that moment—was him.

This isn't the rest of your life, she told herself. *It's just now....*

It didn't have to alter anything in the future. It wouldn't maintain the chaos or disruption that had been in play for so long now in her life. It wouldn't—it couldn't—change anything as long as she didn't let it….

As long as she made sure it *was* just tonight. That it was just about doing what she wanted here and now, and only here and now.

And if she did that, then why not…

Jenna had only to tip her chin slightly upward in order to kiss Ian.

If he was surprised, he didn't show it. He kissed her in response, without hesitation, but also without escalating that kiss beyond what she'd initiated.

So Jenna kicked it up a notch herself, parting her

lips, glad that he parted his, too. His hand at her nape went from a light, consolation rub to a firmer grasp. She thought that while he might be restraining himself, he wasn't giving any indication for her to stop.

And she didn't. She went on kissing him, she raised a hand to his chest, she parted her lips farther, and she even let her tongue tease the very edges of his lips.

Apparently there was only so much he could endure with restraint, though, because when she did that, his other arm came around her and he pulled her nearer. Near enough for her breasts to brush his chest and make her realize that her nipples were already taut against the built-in bra of the bridesmaid dress. Taut and eager to be back in contact with him.

But she didn't do anything to accomplish that. Instead she just concentrated on kissing him, losing track of whose mouth opened wider first, whose tongue made the bolder move and became more brazenly playful, who deepened that kiss and made it more sensual.

Because regardless of which of them led and which of them followed, that was still where things went. She found her other arm wrapped around Ian, her head in the cradle of his hand when it moved into her hair, her knees partially on his lap.

What they'd shared the night before had only whetted Jenna's appetite, and it seemed that the same was true for Ian. That kiss became more and more intense, more heated, more sexy than sensual.

Jenna raised both of her hands to the back of Ian's head, holding him firmly, testing the coarse texture of his hair, taking her turn plundering his mouth the same way he plundered hers.

The surface of her skin seemed to come alive, crying out for his touch, for the feel of it on every inch of her, but nowhere as desperately as on her breasts, which were straining against the fabric of her dress.

Ian's arms tightened around her then, pulling her in closer yet, raising her higher up against him as he did and tilting back her head with the mere urging of his thumb and fingers on either side of her face, drawing their mouths apart.

He rained kisses along the arch of her neck, then to the hollow of her throat, where he found an incredibly sensitive spot that she'd never known was sensitive at all.

Tiny flicks of his tongue on that spot turned her on even more. Her shoulders drew back and her breasts rose toward him in silent plea.

A silent plea he answered by bringing one hand around from her back to clasp her breast.

Ah, but she needed that dress out of the way….

She'd made up her mind about this, about giving in to what she wanted tonight, and she couldn't wait any longer.

She covered Ian's hand at her breast for a moment, pressing, holding him to her before she took it away, kept hold of it and got up from the sofa.

But her attempt to make Ian get to his feet, too, didn't work.

He stayed where he was, holding her hand but shaking his head as he looked up at her.

"I don't want to be one of your regrets," he said.

"You won't be. You can't be," she whispered, knowing it was true because she wanted him too badly to ever regret bringing what had started between them to its natural conclusion.

She pulled on his hand again in encouragement, and she could tell he wasn't completely convinced. But that he also couldn't refuse what he wanted as much as she did.

So he got to his feet and let her lead him up the stairs and into her bedroom.

Moonlight reflected off the spring snow that blanketed the ground outside the two large windows in her room. It cast a milky glow that was just enough to see by.

When they reached the foot of the bed, Ian spun her around and brought her against him to kiss her anew. He caught her head in his grasp to brace her against an onslaught that was anything but restrained now.

Mouths were wide open, tongues pillaged and played, cavorted and careened around each other while Ian kicked off his shoes and then freed his other hand from Jenna's so he could unzip her dress.

Jenna saw no reason not to act on her own impulse to unfasten the buttons of his shirt and pull its tails from his pants when she'd reached the waistband.

And once his shirt was open, she couldn't resist slipping both of her hands inside to the hot silk of his chest and around to the broad expanse of his back.

Continuing to kiss her like there was no tomorrow, Ian pulled her arms away just long enough to peel down her dress and let it fall like a curtain around her ankles.

Then he guided her hands back inside his shirt before he wrapped his own arms around her and held her to him—bare breasts to bare chest. He massaged her back and made her sigh with the pleasure not only at his touch, but from having her naked torso against his.

His shirt just seemed in the way, so she removed it and let her hands become familiar with the pure glory of broad shoulders, of bountiful biceps. And if discovering the perfection of his honed pectorals and the solid washboard of his abs led her to the front of his slacks? That just seemed like a sign that it was time for those to go, too. A sign that she shouldn't be the only one of them standing there in nothing but her lace bikini panties.

Delicately, she figured out how his pants were fastened and unfastened them, sliding his zipper down over what was burgeoning behind it.

She felt Ian smile mid-kiss before he took something from his pocket to toss over his shoulder onto the bed. Then he completed her quest, dropping the tuxedo pants and underwear and even taking off his socks without moving his mouth too far from hers.

There was nothing left between them but her panties, so he slipped those off her hips, too. She stepped out of them, and Ian circled her with one arm, unhesitatingly bringing his other hand to her breast again.

That sudden contact took her breath away for a moment. And then she merely gave in to the joy of finally having what she'd been craving since she'd lost it last night—his hand encompassing her breast….

It just felt so good. Big and warm. Strong and infinitely gentle. Kneading and massaging. Tenderly pinching the very tip into diamond hardness that strained for more.

He held her tight as he eased them both onto her

bed—Jenna on her back, Ian on his side, partially covering her, his thigh slung across hers. Their kisses grew urgent and hungry while his hand went from one breast to the other.

Things that had been long asleep inside of her, things she hadn't even known she was capable of feeling, came more to life with every passing moment, every thrust of his tongue, every press of that hand at her breasts.

Jenna raised one of her legs to cover his, twisting slightly so she was facing him, further entwining them as her hands ran over every inch of his back and then lower, finding that his tight rear end felt even better than it looked.

He abandoned their kiss and bent low enough to put his mouth to her breast. To draw her in and amp up the desires he had already awakened in her.

With flicks of his magic tongue to her nipple, tiny nibbles of his teeth, sucking and releasing and bringing her every nerve ending to the surface of her skin, he had her nearly writhing even before his hand began making a trail down her stomach, down one of her thighs and then up again to the juncture of her legs.

She couldn't quiet the moan that sounded deep in her throat when his fingers found her. And she couldn't keep herself from reaching for him, from opening her eyes and studying the magnificence of the man on her bed.

His entire body was a glory of masculinity, sleek sinew and mounds of muscle all working together, turning more taut in response to what she was doing to him, to the strokes and exploration of that thick, hard staff she held within her grasp.

And then neither of them could contain themselves another moment.

Ian reached over on the bed and retrieved the condom he'd taken from his pants' pocket earlier, sheathing himself before he came to her again.

He kissed her—a long, lingering kiss. He caressed a breast in one hand with adoration. Then he rose above her before the weight of his big body pressed her flat to the mattress as he fitted himself between her thighs.

Jenna answered with the invitation of open legs, and once more, her breath caught as he slid into her with such sublime perfection that it was as if she'd been fashioned especially for him.

His tongue came to reclaim hers, too. His hand at her breast teased and tormented her nipple, as he started to move in a slow, rhythmic dance of his hips and hers.

Up and down, in and out, now faster and faster they moved together in harmony, in unison. Passion, intensity mounted, and somewhere along the way they stopped kissing, and Ian's hands found the mattress on either side of her head, lending strength to each thrust and then speed she couldn't match.

Jenna curled her legs over his. Her hips rose to him to fully receive what he was offering, what he was doing to her, all that he was arousing in her.

She clung to the majesty of his back, and what was building inside of her grew and grew until it overtook her, until it washed through her with a blinding burst that was so exquisite that it held her in its grip and sent tiny sounds from her throat as she was suspended in that moment of almost unbearably divine bliss.

So divine that she nearly missed Ian's own surrender to that same peak.

Nearly, but not quite, as his whole body stiffened, and he plunged so deeply into her that it was as if they truly fused into one body, one being, one moment of shared ecstasy that was truly, shockingly, like nothing Jenna had ever experienced before.

Then it all began to ebb. To ease. Gradually. Little by little. Ian's incredible body relaxed and became a welcome weight atop her. He dropped his forehead on the bed beside her ear and kissed her bare shoulder, the heat of his breath brushing her skin like warm cotton.

For a time, neither of them said or did anything while breathing calmed and quieted, while a wonderful sense of satisfaction, of contentment, of repletion seemed to wrap around them.

Then, in a tone that combined awe and mock chastisement, Ian said, "Jenna Bowen. You have secret superpowers."

Jenna laughed. "I do? Yes, I do! But I think you must, too."

"I don't like to brag," he joked, his voice husky with spent passion, "but I think we rocked the world."

"The *whole* world?"

"Mine, anyway…."

Hers, too. But only her body would admit it with a reflexive raise of her shoulders and an involuntary tightening of her arms around him to hold on for a moment before she realized what she was doing and slightly let go.

His response was a pulse inside of her before he slipped free and rolled to his back, scooping one arm underneath her so he could pull her to his side where she rested her head on his chest.

"Can I stay?" he asked quietly.

Forever?

No, he couldn't have meant that. It was just what flashed through her mind, all on its own.

But she knew he meant could he stay the night.

And in truth, she didn't think she could have endured it if he got up and left.

Only she forced flippancy and said, "Sure. I don't have to work tomorrow, you can even have breakfast with us."

"I can sneak out and then ring the doorbell and pretend that's all I came for so Abby won't know," he offered.

Jenna laughed again. "I don't think you need to do that. She's too young for it to matter. And after how in-love-with-you she was tonight, she'll probably be thrilled to have you here when she wakes up. It'll be a treat for her."

"And the night is still young. Maybe there could be a couple more treats for us before that...."

"Really?" Jenna asked because his lovemaking already surpassed what she'd been accustomed to.

"Like I said, you rocked my world. Let's see if you can do it again."

"Oh, good, no pressure."

"Only in the right places," he muttered under his breath as he repositioned them so he could kiss her and start anew...."

Chapter Ten

Monday was strange for Ian.

It started with his watching Jenna sleep and, oddly, enjoying that so much that he spent a long while at it. Then he woke her with multiple kisses to every surface of bare skin exposed above the blanket that he'd pulled over them both after making love to her for the third time Sunday night.

When she was awake, he made love to her for the fourth time. Once they were done and she was resting in his arms again, he wished that they could stay right where they were for days and days. At least…

Then Abby had called to Jenna, and that wish hadn't been granted.

But he'd gone on to watching Jenna make pancakes while he sat at her kitchen table with a pajama-clad Abby cozily perched on his lap.

And that had its own appeal.

Warm country kitchen. Beautiful woman at the stove. Cuddly, adoring baby enthralled with him and with studying his morning beard.

Sure, it had seemed odd to be satisfied with merely watching Jenna sleep. But it seemed equally odd to feel so content in this domestic situation. But again, he wished that they could all stay this way for days and days. At least…

But he had business appointments. And when Jenna got a call from another nurse asking her to take a three-to-eleven shift at the hospital, the face of her day changed. So that second wish wasn't granted, either. After pancakes that tasted better than anything he could ever remember eating, he'd left Jenna—and Abby—behind, taking with him more reluctance and regret at having to do that than he thought it was possible to feel. That had also seemed odd.

The hours that followed had been busy—particularly since the auction of Jenna's farm was on Wednesday. Plus he'd fielded three calls from his father, primarily about Chelsea.

But all through those calls Ian hadn't been able to think about anything but Jenna, and that was when he'd told his father that he wasn't going to see Chelsea again.

That had resulted in a disagreement with his father. But not even that had stopped him from wishing—every bit as badly as he'd been wishing it since the moment he'd left this morning—that he was with Jenna again.

Which had led him not to return to the apartment on the Mackey and McKendrick compound when he finally finished work late that evening. Instead he went to Jenna's place to park in front of her dark farmhouse and make his gazillionth wish of the day—for her to hurry home from the hospital when her shift was over, despite the fact that they hadn't made plans to see each other tonight.

Because something had happened to him since he'd met her. And the last twenty-four hours had made it impossible for him to keep it at bay any longer.

He felt about Jenna the way he'd never felt about anyone. Not even Iris, not even when he'd asked Iris to marry him. It was a realization he'd come to during the course of the day.

He didn't understand it. He only knew that he was completely at its mercy.

Jenna was all he could think about. He wanted to be with her day and night. He wanted to do everything with her. She was *it,* he admitted to himself in the silence of his car, the silence of the night.

He couldn't explain how he knew, but he knew that she was the one person in the universe for him. It was a gut feeling, an inner knowledge, an instinct, something he couldn't exactly put a name to that all boiled down to one thing—knowing without a doubt that they were destined to be together. That they needed to be.

And unlike with Iris or with Chelsea, it didn't have anything at all to do with his father or his father's agenda—in fact it was actually contrary to what his father wanted.

With Jenna, it wasn't about a single thing except his feelings for her—entirely separate from anything, everything, anyone else.

Accepting that as he sat there in his car dumbfounded

him. Nothing and no one had ever hit him like this, and for a moment, he wondered if he'd gone a little crazy.

But he hadn't. His feelings for Jenna were off the charts, and for the first time in his life, everything else finally seemed to have found its rightful place. *He* seemed to have found his rightful place.

With Jenna, everything else fell away, and nothing mattered as much as the two of them and what they had together. He was just himself—not Morgan Kincaid's son, not one of Morgan Kincaid's *adopted* children, not Morgan Kincaid's reflection or right-hand man or hope for the future.

And maybe because of that, he'd reached a different level with Jenna. A level where he had been more open with her than he had been with anyone, ever. A level where he'd found a whole new closeness, a whole new sense of freedom, a whole new intimacy…

"No wonder last night was so good," he muttered to himself when the memory cropped up.

And oh, what a memory it was!

For a moment he was lost in it, in picturing Jenna, in recalling the texture of her skin, the scent of her perfume, the warmth of her body. In wanting to be right back in bed with her…

Just thinking about her made him smile.

Jenna was everything. Serious when she should be serious. Funny when she should be funny. Intelligent and gorgeous and wise and witty and strong and insightful and generous and sexy and sensual and…

And she was the first person he could genuinely, vividly picture—without a single doubt in his mind—going through the rest of his life with.

"Which is really why I'm here tonight," he mused when it sank in.

He was there because every minute that he'd been without her since he'd met her had felt more empty without her in it.

He was there because he needed to know—right now—if they could have the future together that he so vividly saw for them….

"Wow…" he muttered to himself as it all took root in his mind.

Then something else occurred to him.

Her family home loomed in front of him, her family farm, reminding him that what he wanted didn't come without complications.

There was still the issue of her property and the instrumental role he played in Jenna's not being able to give her late father the one thing he'd asked of her—to keep the place a farm.

And there was Abby.

With Jenna came Abby…

And parenthood…

Not when he'd planned—ten years from now.

Not the way he'd planned. Not the traditional course he'd been determined to take, the traditional course that meant he would meet a woman as free of encumbrances as he was, that meant they would fall in love, marry, have a few years alone together and then start a family of their own making.

In fact, what he was picturing with Jenna was exactly what he'd planned *not* to do. Exactly the way he *hadn't* wanted to become a parent, because he would be a parent to a child who could well feel all the same things he'd felt growing up.

But it was *Abby*....

Cute, cuddly, lovable Abby who had sort of adopted him already…

Abby.

The more he thought about her, the more the fact that they didn't share blood ties began to seem less important.

Abby had latched on to him, anyway. And it was nice. It felt good. Good to have her look up at him with those big, trusting eyes of hers, to have her reach her chubby little arms out to him when she wanted him to hold her, to have her climb up on his lap. It had all spurred something in him, he thought now, when he realized that lurking behind his feelings for Jenna were some fledgling feelings for Abby, too.

He'd known all along that he liked the baby girl. But now, when he analyzed what she'd stirred in him, he recognized protective feelings. Nurturing feelings. Feelings that probably qualified as parental…

That seemed so weird. As weird as seeing Hutch with a kid. As weird as Hutch himself had said it was to find himself a father.

But now Ian could actually start to envision himself stepping into that role with Abby. Doing exactly what he'd been doing with Abby when he'd escorted her around the wedding, every time he'd helped with her care or held her or played with her.

As much as it fed his soul to be with Jenna, it occurred to him that there also seemed to be some indefinable connection between himself and Abby, too. It didn't matter that there wasn't a biological or genetic link tying them together. An already-existing attachment. An attachment that maybe Abby—with the innocence and purity of a child—had felt herself and simply embraced.

An attachment that his own adoptive parents must have felt for him and Hutch at the start and to Lacey when they'd first adopted her.

And couldn't that—wouldn't that—grow to something stronger if he became a fixture in Abby's life from this early age? Couldn't that connection grow as strong as the bonds birth parents and children felt?

His own parents had always told him and his siblings that what they felt for them was no different than what any birth parents felt for their children. That they thought they loved them even more because they'd chosen them…

His own concerns, his sense that he had to work harder to earn his place with them, the right to the Kincaid name, had come from something inside of him. Not from them, he admitted to himself now. It hadn't even come from the pressures his father had put on him and his brother, because he knew that his father would have put the exact same pressures on any biological child.

But what about Abby?

How could he prevent her from feeling the way he'd felt growing up?

He hated the thought of her ever feeling as if she needed to work harder to deserve anything he gave her. To go to extreme lengths to please him.

But maybe Ian and his siblings were a special case because his father—with all his good intentions—had made such a public cause of their adoptive status. Making them feel different.

Maybe if the fact that he wasn't Abby's birth father was taken more in stride, it wouldn't matter as much to the little girl as it had to him.

He wasn't sure. He hoped so.

But before Ian could hash through any more, he saw car lights coming down the road.

His pulse picked up speed.

Jenna.

She was what mattered.

Jenna and Abby and the three of them being together.

The mere thought of that made the complications fade into the background for him.

Jenna and Abby and the three of them being together—that was what he wanted, that was what he was going after.

And he was willing to do whatever it took to make it happen….

It was shortly before midnight when Jenna finally pulled onto the drive that led to her house.

After next to no sleep the night before, chasing after well-rested Abby who wouldn't nap, then working a busy shift at the hospital, she was beat.

And yet, the very minute she spotted Ian's car parked in front of the farmhouse, she perked up.

There hadn't been any arrangement to see him tonight. She hadn't heard from him since he'd left this morning. And while she had gone through the day and evening in a sort of rosy glow after spending the previous night with him, she'd still kept in mind that she'd given herself permission to make love just the one night. Just one night that wouldn't take her off the path she'd set for herself.

But the instant she saw his car, the instant she had the chance to see him again, all of that flew out of her head and what remained was merely the rosy glow and the excited hope that tonight might be spent the way last night had been....

He got out of his car as she pulled up beside it. He looked as wonderful as ever in jeans, a turtleneck sweater and a leather bomber jacket that gave him a hint of bad-boy appeal.

"Hi," she whispered when he stepped up to open her door the minute her engine was off.

"Hi," he answered at a normal volume, smiling a knowing sort of smile that she didn't quite understand.

But rather than addressing it, she nodded over her shoulder and put an index finger to her lips to let him know to be quiet.

Abby had been asleep when she'd picked her up from Meg's house, and the baby had remained asleep through the short drive home. Jenna didn't want to wake her. Especially now.

"I'll get her," Ian whispered. He came around to open the rear passenger door and leaned in to release the baby carrier while Jenna got out of the car.

Neither of them said anything as they went into the house, even as Ian led the way up the stairs to the nursery.

Once they were there, he set the carrier on the floor beside the crib.

He did it gently, without jostling Abby, and there

wasn't a sound to wake her, but the baby raised heavy eyelids anyway, saw him, smiled and said a sleepily pleased, "Un…"

"Sleep tight, Abby," Ian whispered to her, and the baby immediately closed her eyes again.

The whole thing made Jenna smile as she unbuckled Abby from the car seat straps, removed her coat and lifted her into the crib.

Abby turned on her side, curled into a little ball and continued sleeping as Jenna ran a loving hand over her head and kissed her forehead.

Then Jenna stood up straight, motioned toward the door and led Ian out.

They both took off their coats as they retraced their path down the stairs. Jenna left hers on the newel post at the foot of the steps.

She was still wearing her navy blue scrubs, her hair was in the ponytail she'd put it in before work. As Ian hung his bomber jacket on one of the pegs behind the front door, she was wondering if, instead of coming back downstairs, she should have taken him into her bedroom, into her bathroom, into her shower….

But she refrained from suggesting that—just yet—and said, "Are you hungry? Would you like a glass of wine?"

He shook his head, clasped her hand in his and led her into the living room. "I just want to talk," he said.

Had he come to tell her that what had happened between them last night was never going to happen again?

Jenna had been telling herself that all day, but she froze slightly inside at the idea that Ian might be here to say out loud what she'd been thinking. Keeping her cool, she sat down next to him on the couch. Ian took her hand in both of his and stared into her eyes.

The way someone might if they were delivering bad news…

Jenna steeled herself and reminded herself that it was for the best.

"I thought I was coming out here tonight just to see you," he began, as he gazed down at their intertwined hands. He rubbed the back of hers with one of his thumbs. "But while I waited, I had time to think and there's more to it than that." He looked into her face. "More to everything between you and me—or am I in my own fantasy world here?"

She didn't know where this was going, and it made her slightly nervous. But there was also another, underlying feeling that prompted her to say, "No, I don't think you're in your own fantasy world. We've… Things have been… Yes, there's been something pretty remarkable between us."

"Yeah…." he agreed in a way that made her sure he was thinking about the night before. A way that made her smile at the memory, too.

"The thing is," he went on then, "since the minute I laid eyes on you, something has been different, and I finally figured out that it's everything—everything with you is different."

Jenna listened as he told her what he'd thought about and concluded as he'd waited for her to get home—that she was It for him, that they were meant to be together.

And the more he talked, the more stunned she became. The more thrilled and excited and tempted. And the more uneasy…

Then he said, "I know Abby comes with the package—"

Abby...

"—but I did some thinking about that, too. Before you and Abby, when I thought about kids in general, I wanted to put them off. But when I thought about Abby—" He smiled warmly, the way Jenna had seen him smile at the baby. "I'm as crazy about her as I am about you, and I promise you I will never do anything to make her feel the way I felt about being adopted. And if she ever begins to feel second-best because she's adopted, I'll move heaven and earth to change her mind so she can take me for granted—"

"You *want* to be taken for granted?" Jenna asked, not completely grasping the full implication of his statement but finding some humor in it.

"Yeah, when it comes to Abby, I do," he confirmed.

But again Jenna thought, *Abby...*

Yes, there was Abby. Abby who Ian had said he was willing to take on—which Jenna assumed meant to raise as his own child. To parent. To be a father to.

But Jenna had only just begun to be Abby's mom. And she and Abby were in the midst of so much turmoil, so much transition with the loss of J.J., then Jenna's parents, now the farm.

Before Ian—even since Ian had come on the scene—Jenna had been determined to find some calm for herself and Abby, to put some foundation beneath them so they could get their footing, so they could settle in together as a family, as mother and daughter.

Now Ian was talking about something entirely different. About him being a part of that. That was very different from what Jenna had planned.

She wasn't sure that was what was best for Abby. For her.

Adding more change, more upheaval, didn't seem like anything to put in the pro column….

But Jenna hadn't formed any words to express this, when Ian said, "Then there's my father, and that makes a much bigger hornet's nest…"

Jenna's uneasiness tripled, overshadowing the thrilled, excited, tempted feelings she'd had.

His father...

Ian went on to talk about the farm, about being unsure how to handle that, how to handle his father, the auction, the training center, but once more Jenna's mind was wandering. Reeling.

Ian's father...

Warning alarms were shrieking in Jenna's mind. Would Ian have to choose between his father's interests and hers? Which would he choose? Jenna saw the similarity to her ex-husband and his deference to his mother. There was the potential for history repeating itself.

Plus, Morgan Kincaid was also Ian's boss. Ian's livelihood depended on doing what his father wanted.

What if she did get involved with Ian? That didn't change what had always gone on with his father. It didn't change what drove Ian any more than being married to Ted had changed what drove Ted.

So wouldn't she be in the same position? Wouldn't what she wanted, what she needed—and consequently, what Abby wanted or needed—come up second on the list of what was important? Second on the list of what had to be done?

Wouldn't what she and Abby wanted or needed end up sacrificed to Ian's goals exactly the way time with her family had once been sacrificed to Ted's pursuits?

It seemed to Jenna that the answer to that was yes. That if doing Morgan Kincaid's bidding meant living in Billings—or anywhere else—she and Abby would be expected to pick up and move. That if doing Morgan Kincaid's bidding meant anything that conflicted with what she or Abby wanted or needed, they would be expected to suck it up while Ian did that bidding.

Suddenly Jenna felt guilt—for having neglected her parents, for not having been around enough to have seen the signs of their failing health, the signs that the farm was in jeopardy.

She couldn't allow anything like that to ever happen again, with Abby. She couldn't put either of them in a position where Abby might have to take a backseat to Ian's mission to please his father.

And that's what she saw in any future with him.

He was still talking about his father, about how furious his father was, about how he intended to wait until Morgan Kincaid arrived in Northbridge the next day to tell him about Jenna.

All of what Ian was proposing would definitely take her off track—precisely what she'd told herself last night wouldn't happen.

And she couldn't let it happen now.

Could she?

For a moment she wavered.

Ian was there, looking incredible—more handsome

than any man had the right to be. Looking into his eyes was like peering at a cloudless sky reflected off a frozen pond.

He was still holding her hand in both of his, enveloping it with a tender strength, a warmth that seeped through her skin and heated her all the way through, reminding her of what it was like to feel his touch over every inch of her body.

And the simple truth was that she wanted him. She wanted to be with him. She wanted them to be together. Together like they had been last night. Together like they had been at his sister's wedding and the rest of the time since they'd met. Together…

But in the end, she pulled her hand from his. Stretched her spine straighter and moved an inch or so away from him, enough for him to pause in what he'd been saying.

And that was when she heard herself announce, "Last night was a one-time thing."

Before he could say anything, she rushed on.

"I'm not ready for more than that. Since we haven't found a buyer for the farm who will honor our wishes, Abby and I need to leave this place where I grew up, where she was born, the only home she's ever known. I'm a new parent. Abby and I need time to get our bearings, time to really become a family for each other. And you have your own family—your father, your brother, a nephew—you have your work—which is probably going to turn my farm into a training center…" Her voice cracked. "There's just…too much."

"There's a lot," he agreed. "But we can work it out."

Jenna almost frantically shook her head. "Working it out means someone has to make sacrifices, and that someone will end up being me. And Abby. I can't do that. I won't do that."

"I won't ask you to. I like Northbridge. I have family of my own here now. It's close enough to Billings for me to commute when I need to. With the training facility and the offices for the Monarchs here, I'll be working more than half the time from this town. You won't need to sacrifice anything."

He seemed so certain of that. But Jenna wasn't buying it.

"There might be compromises," he added then, "but I promise you that I will never make you or Abby play second fiddle—to anything or anyone."

Jenna shook her head again, slower now, but more firmly. "No. Abby and I need to stay on our course. And you and I…"

Why was it so difficult—almost impossible—for her to say that she and Ian couldn't go on together?

She swallowed a huge lump in her throat. "You and I had some fun, but we have to get back to the day-to-day. You to yours. Me to mine. We have to go our separate ways…."

Ian frowned, his handsome face dark and stormy. He looked as if he couldn't believe what she was saying.

"You know, I was there last night, Jenna," he said then. "That wasn't just 'some fun.' It was fun—don't get me wrong. But you and I both know that there was more to it. That there's more to you and me. Too much to just blow it off and 'go our separate ways.'"

"That's how I want it," she insisted, pushing stubbornly through even as she was waffling inside, because this *wasn't* what she wanted, it was just what she had to do.

"You want me to get up right now, walk out the door and pretend nothing happened? Pretend that we didn't tap into something so damn amazing here that it shouldn't just be left behind? That it shouldn't *ever* be left behind?"

"That's what I want," she said in a voice too soft to support the words but with shoulders drawn back to prove she meant it. "Abby and I just need to be Abby and I…."

And never had she felt the kind of pain she felt at that moment when she was freezing him out.

But still she convinced him, because with eyebrows arched in dismay and that supple mouth of his set in stony anger, Ian stood.

"This is really, genuinely, what you want?" he asked skeptically.

She nodded because she didn't trust her voice.

Ian said nothing to that. He merely turned, went into the entry, grabbed his bomber jacket off the peg and walked out.

But he closed the door quietly after himself, so as not to wake Abby—it was something Jenna took note of. Something she hadn't expected him to do when she'd just made him mad. A small, caring consideration at the worst of times that only caused her to want him all the more.

And it was something that, for no reason she could explain, put her over the edge.

She buried her face in the couch cushion to muffle the sob that accompanied a flood of tears.

Chapter Eleven

The farm was off the auction block.

Jenna only found out late Tuesday evening when the Realtor called. Marsha Pinkell said that she'd seen that the Bowen farm was no longer up for auction and wanted to know if Jenna was going to continue to list the farm for sale.

"What do you mean the farm isn't on the auction block anymore?" Jenna asked.

"I assumed you must have raised the money and paid the taxes," Marsha Pinkell said. "All I know is that your place was one of the three going up for auction tomorrow and when I was double-checking the time just now, I saw that your farm had been removed from the schedule. The old Wilkerson house and that run-down barn just outside of town will be auctioned tomorrow, but your property won't be."

Jenna still wasn't sure she'd heard the Realtor right.

But since Ian's midnight visit the night before, she'd been in a sort of haze of misery. She'd lost hours Tuesday, sitting on the floor with Abby, staring vacantly at nothing while the baby played beside her and she wondered if she'd done the right thing by turning down Ian. And if she *had* done the right thing, then why did it feel so bad…?

So now it took Jenna some concentrated effort to understand the situation.

Her farm wasn't being auctioned. And she hadn't sold the place.

That could only mean that the taxes had been paid.

Marsha broke into her thoughts with a question. "Are you still interested in selling?"

"I'll have to get back to you," was the only answer Jenna could give before she hung up.

And stared into space again.

The single thing that would have kept the farm from being auctioned off tomorrow was to pay the taxes her father had fallen behind on. The town fund had never reached the forty thousand dollars it would have taken, so it hadn't come from there.

Somehow she just knew Ian had paid them….

Maybe she was wrong. Maybe she was jumping the gun.

Because why would Ian pay her taxes? Paying her taxes didn't give him any rights to the place. It didn't buy it for the Kincaid Corporation—only purchasing it through the auction or directly from her would have accomplished that.

And with her taxes paid, she now had complete control again. No one could get their hands on this property unless she sold it to them. Without the tax debt, she didn't need to sell. And even if she decided to anyway, she could stand her ground on the contingency that the place remain a working farm—which meant that she would never cave in to the Kincaid Corporation's turning it into a training center.

Ian knew that. So if he paid the taxes, Ian's father would be mad. Furious. Probably outraged to lose the property he wanted for his football team…

So maybe it wasn't Ian.

Maybe there was some other charitable soul who had stepped in at the last minute. Someone who wanted to remain anonymous. Some secret Good Samaritan…

Except that deep down, Jenna still thought that Ian had done this.

And if he had, she didn't know what to think of it. How to feel about it. What it meant. What he might want in exchange…

There was only one way to find out.

She had to talk to him.

Or was she just looking for an excuse to see him?

She took a deep breath, closed her eyes and blew it out—long and slow—trying to clear her head.

She did want to see him. Desperately. There was no doubt about it.

And now she had very good reason to do just that. She needed to find out if he'd paid her taxes. And she didn't want to just call and ask. If he'd invested forty thousand dollars in her farm, they needed to talk about that face-to-face.

Cell phone still in her hand from her previous call,

Jenna dialed her usual teenage babysitter to come and stay with Abby.

Then she took a look at herself. After a call to Meg at dawn, her best friend had rushed over to spend the morning consoling her and comforting her. So Meg had seen her in her ragged sweats, make-up-less, her hair flat and stringy. But Jenna didn't want anyone else to see her like that.

Especially Ian.

"Come on, Ab, I have to take a quick shower," she informed the baby, scooping her up from the floor and making a beeline upstairs.

With Abby playing safely in her crib, Jenna had a quick shower and a quick shampoo. After drying off, she set Abby on the bedroom floor with more toys and slipped into clean jeans and a lace camisole top that showed from beneath the navy blue, scoop-neck T-shirt she wore over it.

Because her hair was freshly washed, and she was short on time, she bent over at the waist so her head was upside down and did a fast blow-dry, scrunching the long locks as she did.

Abby loved the blow dryer, so Jenna had to spend a few minutes aiming it at the fifteen-month-old—who pinched her eyes shut and giggled at the sensation. Then Jenna turned it off, distracting Abby from her protests by diverting her attention to the closet, where Jenna got a pair of ballet-slipper shoes to put on.

She brushed her hair and let the waves fall freely around her shoulders. A little blush, a little mascara, a faintly colored lip gloss, and she was ready. She carried Abby downstairs just as the babysitter got there.

Jenna usually had Abby ready for bed when the sitter arrived. But tonight she gave the teenager instructions for putting the infant to sleep. Then she kissed Abby goodbye and rushed out to her car.

Ian might have paid the taxes...

What did that mean?

That was what she kept thinking as she drove to the Mackey and McKendrick compound.

The lights were on in the main house when she got there. It was no surprise. Before Meg had left her this morning, her friend had tried to persuade Jenna to come to her house with her so Jenna wouldn't be alone in her misery.

Jenna had rejected that idea, worried that being that near to Ian would only make things more difficult. Meg had understood but said she'd be home all afternoon and evening if Meg changed her mind.

But Jenna was too eager, too intent on getting to Ian now to stop at Meg's first. Instead she drove around the main house and parked near the garage that stood beneath the studio apartment that Ian was using.

Turning off the car engine and lights, Jenna got out and hurried up the wooden staircase that ran along the side of the garage, her ballet-slipper shoes making no noise.

Still, she was two steps from the landing at the top before she realized that there were voices coming from inside the apartment.

Loud voices.

Loud voices of two men.

She froze in her tracks, recalling in that instant

that Morgan Kincaid had been due in town today or tomorrow for the auction.

That had to be who Ian was with. And there was no way she was going to walk in on father and son shouting at each other.

But just as she turned to go back down the steps it was Ian's voice that sounded loud enough for her to hear and—right or wrong—Jenna froze to listen.

"Look, it's done. You can trust me or not—it's your choice. But I've paid the Bowen taxes out of my own pocket so the farm won't be up for auction. With that done, Jenna Bowen won't sell the property to us. That takes the Bowen place out of the equation and leaves the McDoogal place—"

"The McDoogal place is seven acres too big and a hell of a lot more money!"

"I told you I can get them down on the price. I can also try to sell the extra acreage to the surrounding farms to make up some of the cost and get us down to no more than the seventeen acres we would have been getting with the Bowen farm. This way the Monarchs can come into town with their heads held high, not having half of Northbridge hating us for profiting on the hard times of one of their own. Or I can bow out and you can get someone else to do my job. It's your call, but that's the best that's going to get done here."

"Because you got blinded by some woman!" Morgan Kincaid yelled.

"That's right, I did," Ian countered. "And I did what I needed to do for her."

"You could have had Chelsea Tanner and the team could have had a fast ticket to permanent sponsorship from her father! We could have had the property we needed and paid a song for it! Instead what do we have? What do *you* have? Nothing! The woman doesn't even want you!"

She'd go see Meg, Jenna decided when she heard that and—feeling even worse than she had before—she silently ran down the steps and across the yard to her best friend's back door.

"I only know that Morgan Kincaid got here about two hours ago, and that there have been some raised voices coming from the apartment ever since," Meg said when Jenna told her what she'd just overheard.

"They've been at it for *two hours?*" Jenna lamented. She was standing at Meg's kitchen sink, spying out the window to keep an eye on the garage apartment.

Meg was standing beside her, her gaze trained in the same direction although they could see Ian or Morgan Kincaid only when they passed by the apartment window that faced the main house.

"Two hours," Meg confirmed. "He and Ian were supposed to have dinner with Chase and Hadley but Hadley said Ian called it off just before his father got here."

"Because he knew his father wouldn't take it well when he told him he'd paid my taxes…."

"It looks like he was right."

"And now he could lose his job and this could cause another family rift and—"

"And apparently it was worth it to Ian," Meg said pointedly. "Apparently *you* were worth it to Ian."

Jenna grimaced. "Don't make me feel any worse than I already do."

"I don't want to…" Meg said. "But now you know that Ian is his own man."

Over coffee and crying that morning Jenna had told her friend everything—including her concerns about Ian being no different from Jenna's ex when it came to living his life to please someone else.

"I can't believe," Meg was saying, "that standing up to the wrath of Morgan Kincaid is any easier than it would have been for Ted to stand up to his mother and tell her he didn't want to be a doctor. But Ian did this. For you. Even after you turned him down."

"You don't want to make me feel any worse than I already do, but you're going to anyway?" Jenna said wryly.

Meg shrugged. "Maybe a little bit. I just don't want you to do something you'll be sorry for later, Jen. I know a lot has happened to you in the last eleven months. I know you really, really need things to settle down, for you and for Abby. I know you think adding Ian to the mix just means more chaos and upheaval—and at first, it might. I know all the reasons you sent him packing last night—you told them to me this morning. I'm just not sure you're doing what's going to ultimately make you happy."

She certainly hadn't been happy since sending Ian packing….

But her reasons still seemed valid, and she was glad when Logan popped his head into the kitchen to tell Meg that Tia was ready for them to read her bedtime story and tuck her in for the night.

"Go," Jenna urged her friend. "I just want to wait a little and see if Morgan leaves so I can talk to Ian."

Meg didn't argue. She merely reached out an arm to give Jenna a bolstering hug and then left Jenna to continue staring up at the apartment. Thinking.

Oh, how she'd hated hearing what Ian's father had said about how he'd paid the taxes and put himself in this position all for someone who didn't want him!

It was so, so not true!

She did want him. Horribly. She just hadn't thought she should give in to her feelings.

Obviously her best friend didn't agree with that position.

Am I wrong? Jenna asked herself.

She couldn't deny that, yes, it seemed that she had been mistaken in thinking that Ian was like her ex-husband, that Ian wasn't his own man, that pleasing his father would come first with him.

Ian had paid her taxes and taken her out of harm's way—not only at his own financial expense, but to his own detriment when it came to dealing with his father and thwarting what the great Morgan Kincaid wanted, too.

She supposed that there were indications along the way that Ian was different than Ted—Ian *had* said that he'd played football because he loved the game, which meant that he hadn't done it solely to please his father. And he had stayed with the sport on the business side, even after leaving the Kincaid Corporation when he and his father and brother had had their disagreement.

That disagreement had been a good example of Ian standing his ground when Morgan Kincaid had overstepped his bounds. Ian had had the guts, the backbone, the strength to step away from his father and his job.

To go out on his own, to leave behind that father whose approval he valued rather than take what his father had been dishing out.

Ted would never have done any of that.

And now, paying her taxes, not letting his father have her farm for the Monarchs' training center? That was standing up to his father yet again in a very big way.

On behalf of someone who had rejected him.

On behalf of someone who had been so sure she—and ultimately, Abby—would be sacrificed instead.

Well, he'd proven her wrong. He'd been the one to make the sacrifice. The greater sacrifice.

And she just felt awful….

But that hadn't been the only reason she'd said no to him, she reminded herself.

There *was* Abby. But didn't the fact that baby Abby was so willing and eager to have Ian around mean that it would actually be better to let him become a part of their little family now, when Abby was most open to including him?

He'd already been nothing but kind and caring and loving toward the baby. He'd already shown he'd be a good father.

Because Ian was just a good guy. A great guy, Jenna admitted.

And Abby wasn't the only one of them who adored him…

The underlying truth was that Jenna adored him, too.

The moment she thought that, a big black town car drove up to the compound, coming to a stop near the stairs that led up to the garage apartment. The apartment door opened and out came Morgan Kincaid.

From what Jenna could see of his expression in the dim light, the former football star didn't look any too appeased as he barreled down the stairs and into the car, past the driver, who had gotten out to hold the rear door open for him.

The driver quickly closed the door, slid behind the wheel again and put the car into motion, going back the way he'd come.

When they were gone, Jenna's gaze rose once more to the top of the stairs.

Ian was standing out on the landing now, in the cold, watching as his father was driven off.

Then he spotted Jenna standing at Meg's kitchen window….

Chapter Twelve

Jenna's mind was racing as she hurried across the yard to the garage. Ian merely stood where he was on the landing, watching her come.

Once she climbed the stairs and was facing him, she still didn't know what to say, where to begin.

A simple hello seemed too mundane at that point, and instead she found herself blurting out, "I came to talk to you, but your father was here and I could tell things were…heated…so I went over to Meg's to wait until you were alone. But if you have too much to deal with right now—"

Ian cut her off with the shake of his head and motioned for her to go into the apartment ahead of him.

She did, appreciating the warmth of the room because she'd forgotten to put on a coat in her rush to leave Meg's.

Then, only a few feet inside, she turned to watch Ian

come into the apartment and close the door. He put his back to it and crossed his arms over his broad chest, frowning slightly at her.

"What can I do for you?" he asked in a deep, serious voice, sounding as if he were a little weary underneath it all, as if he was merely resigned to having what he thought was going to be his second unpleasant encounter of the night.

But for a split second Jenna was just glad to be in the same room with him again, and she feasted on her view of him in jeans and a black cashmere crewneck.

Gawking at him wasn't why she was there, however, and after reminding herself of that, she got right to the point.

"I know you paid my taxes," she said bluntly.

"It wasn't a big deal," he countered, as if it had been nothing.

"It's a very big deal. In more ways than one," Jenna declared, deciding in that instant to just jump in with both feet and tell him all she'd sorted through since overhearing a portion of his argument with his father.

She told him that her own bad past experience had led her to misjudge him, to compare him to her ex-husband and file him away in that same category. She told him that she had been wrong to do that, that she knew now that he wasn't anything like Ted, that he would never sacrifice her or Abby to what his father wanted, and she apologized for ever believing that of him.

As she spoke, she realized that she'd been glancing everywhere but his face, his eyes, because she'd been too afraid of what she might see there.

So she altered her gaze, forcing herself to look at him squarely.

But his expression hadn't changed—it remained a blank slate as he stood there, merely listening.

It wasn't encouraging. But since she had more to say, she went on.

"It's been nice, it's felt good, to have it be the three of us," she told him, explaining how her thinking had altered on that count, too. How maybe the speed with which things had happened between them had frightened her. How maybe she'd even been a little selfish when it came to Abby. She'd wanted so much for her and Abby to bond, and she didn't want Ian to interrupt that. Certainly she'd worried that including Ian in the mix would be an additional distraction just when she was striving for calm.

"But maybe now is the best time for us to start a new family…for you and I…for you to join us. For us to become a family of three instead of a family of two…" she concluded with a question in her voice because she still couldn't judge his reaction.

Not that she could blame him if he had changed his mind. Because he was angry or disgusted with her, because he'd had second thoughts about being with her, let alone taking on a child, too.

Then, feeling uncomfortable, she added with a nervous sort of laugh, "After all, Abby seems to have picked you for us…."

"You're going to let Abby do your matchmaking?" Ian finally said into a silence she wasn't sure would ever end.

"She seems to have really good taste in men," Jenna claimed.

And that was when Ian finally smiled, and as drop-dead gorgeous as she thought that face of his was, it had never looked as wonderful to her as it did then, giving her a glimmer of hope that she hadn't ruined things between them.

"You've had a lot slung at you for a long time, Jenna," he said. "And I know I came at you with both barrels myself, right in the middle of losing your farm, your home, your parents. All while you were setting up housekeeping for yourself and Abby. I hit you with too much—I saw that—and I never wanted to make things more complicated for you. I wanted them to be simpler—"

"So you paid my taxes."

He shrugged that off.

"I'll pay you back," she swore. "It'll take time, but—"

Ian shook his head. "I paid your taxes to *give* you time. And options. You can stay in the house and work the farm. Or you can stay in the house and hire the farm work out. Or you can keep the place up for sale with any conditions you want attached and wait for a buyer who will accept those conditions. Or you can sell just the land to be farmed by someone else so you at least have a place to live."

"I do have a lot of options now," she agreed. But then she said very quietly, "What about you? Are you still one of them?"

"I am," he said just that simply, coming away from the door and stepping up close in front of her to slide one hand under her hair to her nape.

The feel of his touch was exactly what she needed—

she nearly melted right there. She swayed slightly in his grip and said, "I'll still repay you…."

"Or the forty thousand could be my dowry. Or my buy-in."

Jenna smiled. "Your dowry?"

His only answer to that was a grin. "My vote—if I have one—is that we keep the whole property, hire out the farm work, but do some renovations on the house. That way you and Abby can stick to your roots and not lose any more than the two of you already have, but we can update the place a little."

"And you'd be part of the update?" she teased him.

"The best part," he joked with bravado.

No argument there, Jenna thought.

But that reminded her that he'd been arguing earlier with his father.

"What about your dad and your job? Do I need to teach you to farm for a living?"

"My father is unhappy with me at the moment but he'll get over it, and yes, I do still have a job. My family has already had to put things back together once before—Hutch is only now coming back into the fold after our last big blow up. But this time, my father ultimately saw that I wanted you bad enough to do whatever it took, and he accepted it. Ranting and raving about it—that's his way—but he accepted it."

"So you wanted me bad enough to do whatever it took," she repeated with some bravado of her own. "What else would you have done?"

The hint of challenge made him laugh. "Maybe just this…" he said before he kissed her. It was the kiss of a rogue—mouth open from the start, tongue claiming hers, bold and brash and brazenly branding her as his.

Which Jenna sanctioned and seconded. Her lips parted, she met him on equal ground.

As he pulled her closer, Jenna snaked her arms under his and splayed her hands across his massive back. It sank in that they'd weathered this storm, that they'd actually touched on plans for the future….

But thoughts of the future were shoved aside by what was happening in the moment as the fires they'd lit before blazed between them again.

That kiss grew hotter and hotter, more and more intense as passion flamed and flourished, and clothes began to be shed, as hands began to explore and arouse and delight.

Jenna was in nothing but bikini panties and a lacy bra when their kiss took an intermission so Ian could sweep her up in his arms and carry her to the bed.

Standing beside it once he'd playfully laid her there, he dropped what remained of his own clothes—his already-unfastened and unzipped jeans—while Jenna devoured the sight of the muscular, well-honed torso and biceps that made her mouth water, then took a longing look at the magnificence of the rest of him bared to her, nearly moaning at just how glorious a vision it was.

Joining her on the bed, he made short work of disposing of what little she was still wearing, too, before he recaptured her mouth with his.

They made love with an abandon that Jenna had never known. With a freedom born of the certainty that they were sealing what was between them when they reached a pinnacle that was so explosive it left them depleted and weak and able to do nothing but hold each other while they caught their breath in an almost blinding afterglow.

That was how they remained for a while, bodies still united, Jenna lying atop Ian as he ran those big hands of his up and down her bare back again and again.

Then, in a raspy whisper, he said, “I love you, Jenna.”

“I love you, too, Ian. More than I can ever tell you,” Jenna responded as naturally as the feelings that had taken root within her.

“And you’ll marry me?” he asked.

“I will,” she answered with a replete smile, her cheek resting on his chest. Then she craned her head back so she could look up at him and said, “But we’ll have to come up with a story for how you proposed that doesn’t have us naked in bed—how can we tell the grandkids that!”

“We’ll say that I rushed you late one night, and you turned me down, then you thought about what you’d be missing—” he quickly stole a kiss “—and you knew you couldn’t live without it.”

Jenna laughed again. “That hardly cleans it up.”

“Okay, how about this—I rushed you late one night because I knew I couldn’t live without you and you turned me down—”

“Then you showed me how much you cared about me and Abby, and when I came to talk to you about it—”

“You couldn’t keep your hands off me, we ended up in bed and—”

“This story is still going to take some fine-tuning.”

“We’ll work on it,” he assured her. “But for now, I’m guessing Abby is either over with Meg and Logan or at your place with a babysitter—”

"I think it's our place now, isn't it?"

The smile that spread across his handsome face showed how much he liked hearing that.

"And I think we should get dressed and go home to her."

Jenna couldn't help another smile of her own, pleased by the thought of the two of them going home to Abby.

"You'll make a great dad."

"We'll make a great family," he amended, bringing his head forward to give her a long, heartfelt kiss. "You and me and Abby and the other kids we'll have—because we will have other kids, too. Right?" he asked when that kiss ended.

"I can see in the crystal ball that we will, yeah," she assured him.

"And they'll be our kids exactly the same way Abby is our kid."

"And they'll all take us for granted," Jenna teased him.

"Good!" he said victoriously.

Jenna merely smiled at that. "I do love you." She whispered it this time, because the happy tears she was holding back were quieting her voice.

"I do love you," Ian echoed.

And even though it was time to get up and go home, Jenna stayed where she was for another moment, savoring what she'd found with Ian and thinking about those dark clouds he'd said she'd been under since J.J.'s death.

Even in the black of night now, she knew those clouds had lifted. That Ian had lifted them. That with him to share her life, they were gone for good.

"Come on, let's go home," he urged with another kiss to the top of her head.

After hugging him tightly for a split second, Jenna let go of him so they could get up and return to the place that had brought them together.

The place where they would live out the rest of their lives.

Peacefully, joyfully, contentedly.

And for that, she didn't need a crystal ball to be sure.

* * * * *

Special Offers

Every month we put together collections and longer reads written by your favourite authors.

Here are some of next month's highlights—and don't miss our fabulous discount online!

On sale 18th January

On sale 1st February

On sale 1st February

Find out more at
www.millsandboon.co.uk/specialreleases

Visit us Online

0213/ST/MB399